W9-BSD-465

POCKET LEPRECHAUN STORIES

Gill Books
Hume Avenue, Park West, Dublin 12

www.gillbooks.ie

Gill Books is an imprint of M.H. Gill & Co.

Copyright © Teapot Press Ltd 2016

ISBN: 978-0-7171-6919-1

This book was created and produced by Teapot Press Ltd

Retold by Fiona Biggs
Illustrated by James Lent
Designed by Tony Potter

Printed in Europe by Factor Druk

This book is typeset in Sabon Infant

All rights reserved.

No part of this publication may be copied, reproduced
or transmitted in any form or by any means, without
permission of the publishers.

A CIP catalogue record for this book is available
from the British Library.

5 4 3 2 1

POCKET LEPRECHAUN STORIES

Stories retold by Fiona Biggs
Illustrated by James Lent

Gill Books

Contents

Introduction

He's a span

And a quarter in height,

Get him in sight, hold him tight,

And you're a made man!

'The Lepracaun or Fairy Shoemaker', William Allingham (1824–1889)

Everyone knows about leprechauns, those little men dressed in green or red, with funny hats and bright shiny buckles on their boots, but not very many of us have actually seen one. They like to keep well out of the way of humans, but there are some people who are always looking for them, because all the old stories tell us that every leprechaun has a crock of gold, and if he can be persuaded to give it up, endless riches will be the reward for perseverance.

Leprechauns have just one profession – cobbler – and people usually discover them because they can hear the tap-tapping of their tiny hammers. They always have lots of shoes to mend because one of their favourite pastimes is dancing – they have céilidhs with the other little people almost every night. Leprechauns are great musicians, and will fiddle and pipe until dawn. A leprechaun céilidh is a wonderful sight to behold, but if they know that anyone is watching them, they'll disappear in an instant!

It's well known that leprechauns don't like humans, but that's because we're always trying to get our hands on their gold. In fact, the leprechauns don't need the gold for themselves, but they collect it so that can pay a ransom if anyone captures them. It takes them a long time to make a single gold coin – about a year – and they have to make the coins themselves. They get the gold for this by finding their way into our houses and shaving tiny pieces of gold from our coins and ornaments and jewellery. So if you catch a leprechaun, you should hope that it's an old one – the older he is, the bigger his pot of gold will be. These days, leprechauns usually wear green coats and breeches, but they used to dress in red from head to toe, so if you come across one wearing a tattered red coat, or with a red patch on his breeches, you'll know that he's probably very old and probably very rich.

If you catch a leprechaun, you must hold on to him very tightly and not take your eyes off him; otherwise he'll disappear. Leprechauns have many tricks up their sleeves to make you lose your grip, but, as you'll see in these stories, there are a few things you can do to

make sure you get your prize. You just might end up with the leprechaun's crock of gold if you keep your head and always stay one step ahead of him. Easier said than done!

It might seem that the crock of gold at the end of the rainbow or buried under the hawthorn tree is the real prize, but actually the best thing you can ever do for yourself is perform a good deed for a leprechaun. If you do him a favour, you won't get his crock of gold, but you will get his gratitude, and luck will certainly follow you for the rest of your life. So the next time you think you hear that telltale tap-tap-tap, get ready to be as clever as he is!

A Sting in the Tale

One hot summer's day, Darach was taking a nap in the hedge along the edge of his field, the one by the side of the fairy fort. He always had a good rest there. He found the steady hum of the bees gathering pollen from the summer flowers very soothing. An occasional butterfly flew close to his face, and he batted it away gently without waking up.

After he'd been asleep for a while, he had a dream about a cobbler, tap-tap-tapping away at a pair of broken shoes. When he woke up, stretching, he could still hear the tapping noise from his dream.

'Now, that's very odd,' he thought. 'What would a cobbler be doing in the middle of a field on a hot summer's day?'

The noise stopped for a minute or two, then it started up again – tap, tap, tap. It seemed to be coming from the ditch over to his left. So Darach crept forward very slowly and looked into the ditch. He rubbed his eyes to be sure that he was really seeing what he thought he was seeing.

Sure enough, there in the cool of the ditch, sitting on a large speckled mushroom, was the tiniest little man he had ever seen. His old-fashioned clothes were clean but patched, he was wearing a hat with a big shiny buckle in the middle of it, and he was surrounded by tiny shoes of all shapes and colours. He was working away, not minding anyone or anything, putting new soles on a pair of red dancing shoes.

'Goodness,' thought Darach to himself, pinching his arm to make sure he wasn't still dreaming, 'it's a real live leprechaun!'

He'd listened to all the old stories about the little people, so he knew what to do. He reached out and grabbed the little man in his fist.

'Where is your pot of gold?' he boomed, making the little man cover his ears. 'I need you to show me your gold,' he repeated, a little less loudly.

'What gold?' asked the little man, crossly. 'Sure, how would an honest working person like me have a pot of gold? Can't you see that I'm a shoemaker by trade – and when did you ever see a rich one of those?'

'Do you think I came down in the last shower?' asked Darach. 'I know you're a leprechaun, and I know you have a pot of gold, hidden far away from prying eyes. The shoemaking is just something you do to while away the hours. I want your gold, and I'm not letting you go until you take me to it.'

'All right,' said the little man, sighing. 'I'll take you there. Could you just check under that bush for me? I think I left my boots there.'

'Hah!' said Darach, keeping his eyes glued to the leprechaun. 'You think you can fool me that easily? I'm keeping my eyes on you, or you'll disappear and I'll lose my only chance of becoming rich.'

The little man scowled – he had been foiled by this clever human. There was nothing for it but to lead him to his gold.

'The gold is under that big bush at the top of the hill,' he admitted. 'If you take me there, I'll let you have it. I don't have a choice, do I?' he muttered resentfully.

And so off they went, Darach holding the leprechaun right in front of his eyes so there was no chance that he'd look away and risk losing the gold.

Eventually they got to the top of the hill, a long hot climb on a summer's day. Even though he was very small, the leprechaun seemed to get heavier and heavier with every step Darach took. 'Never mind,' he thought, wiping the perspiration out of his eyes with his free hand, 'soon I'll be rich, really rich! I'll never have to work again!'

'Well,' he said to the leprechaun, when he'd got his breath back after the climb. 'Where's this gold of yours?'

'It's in the bush, of course,' said the leprechaun. 'Why else do you think we've come all this way?'

'Which bit of the bush is it in?' asked Darach suspiciously.

'Oh, right in the middle,' said the leprechaun, looking strangely pleased with himself for a fellow who was about to hand his riches over to a human.

Keeping his eyes firmly glued to the leprechaun, Darach reached into the bush with his free hand and… he got the fright of his life! Instead of grabbing a pot of gold, he'd put his hand right into the middle of a beehive, and the bees, furious at being disturbed, were stinging him. He looked down to see where the hive was and he immediately felt a lightness in his other hand. When he looked up again, his hand was grasping air – the leprechaun had vanished, as all the old stories said he would.

'Not so clever now, not so clever now …' laughed the voice floating back to him on the breeze.

So that was the end of Darach's big chance of getting rich – and he never ate honey again.

A True Story

Brian was a boastful young man, very fond of the sound of his own voice and very sure of his opinions. He'd spend long evenings at the pub, laughing and joking with his friends and telling stories about ghosts and leprechauns and fairies. However, even though he would tell everyone that fairies and little people and leprechauns were all nonsense, he was never too happy when he had to travel home alone along the dark roads after a night out at the pub. Sometimes his loudest protests about fairies and the like were made just before he left the warm cosiness of the pub and set out on the road home alone.

One night, Brian was boasting, as usual, and his booming voice reached into one of the darker corners of the pub.

'You don't believe in the little people?' It was the quavering voice of an old woman.

Brian turned and looked at her.

'Not even leprechauns?' she asked.

'Especially not leprechauns,' said Brian, smirking.

'Well, isn't that a strange thing,' she said. 'Haven't I met one?'

'Now, that I find hard to believe,' laughed Brian. 'Come into the light, why don't you, and tell us all about it.'

The old woman shuffled out of the corner and sat down on a stool next to the fire. Everyone in the pub gathered round, drinks in their hands, to hear what she had to say. Stories were one thing, but this was a real living memory!

'It was when I was a young woman,' she said. 'I was sitting in the garden one lovely summer's day, doing some embroidery and listening to the birds singing and the bees buzzing around the flowers. I remember thinking that the bees were about to swarm.

'It was so warm and lovely that I was just about to doze off, when I heard a strange noise coming from the corner of the garden.'

'What sort of noise?' asked her captivated audience, with one voice.

'Well, it was like the noise a cobbler makes when he's repairing the sole of a shoe – tap, tap, tap.

'I got up off my chair, put my embroidery on the seat and crept up to the corner of the garden that was producing the noise. It got louder as I got closer to the sweet peas. When I got to the edge of the flowerbed, I

carefully parted the flowers and looked into the space underneath the canes. And there, shaded by the leaves, was the tiniest little man I have ever seen! He was all dressed in green, with big shiny buttons on his coat, and he was wearing a black hat with a silver buckle. My ears hadn't deceived me – he was sitting on the ground, hammering nails into a tiny shoe. I knew at once that he was a leprechaun.'

'So what did you do?' asked Brian, who was wondering how on earth the story could be true, although the old woman seemed to be in full possession of her senses.

'Well, I thought it was best to be polite – that always gets you a long way. "Good day," I said. "It's a hot day for the work." "How would you know?" says he. "I'm the one doing it."

'Well, that, as you may imagine, made me angry, so I reached down and grabbed the little man. As soon as I had a hold of him, I asked him to show me where he kept his pot of gold.

'"What gold?" says he. "Where would I get gold? I'm a poor man, working for my living, as you can see. I have no gold. Why would I be working my fingers to the bone if I had a stash of gold? Tell me that!"

'I looked him right in the eye. "Everyone knows leprechauns have a stash of gold," I said. "And I'm not letting you go until you tell me where it is." And I pulled my vegetable knife out of my pocket and scowled at him. "Give me your gold, or I'll cut your ears off!" I ordered in my fiercest voice. The little man looked terrified, and I was so frightened of myself, I almost dropped him!

'"All right," he said. "I'll show you where I keep it, but you'll have to come with me across the fields."

'Now, I knew that I couldn't take my eyes off him. If I did, he'd disappear and I'd be left with no way of finding the gold.

'So off we went across the fields – it was a long way, and it was very hot, so I was walking very slowly. I knew that I couldn't take my eyes off him, and the effort of that was taking all my concentration. Then I heard a loud buzzing just behind me.

'"Your bees are swarming! Your bees are swarming!' said the leprechaun, looking and sounding very alarmed.

'I turned to look, but there was nothing there at all, and when I looked back, my hand was empty. The leprechaun had disappeared, and I was as poor as I had been at the start of the day.'

The old woman sat back and gazed into the fire.

'And that's how I know that leprechauns are real,' she said. 'If ever you meet one, don't believe a word he says, and …'

'Never take your eyes off him!' shouted Brian and his friends.

Cooby the Spotted Cow

There was once a farmer called Diarmuid who had a wife, three children and a fine milk cow called Cooby. Cooby was like one of the family and was very gentle. She was white, with three black spots on her back, and her horns turned in towards her eyes, so you would have known her anywhere.

Diarmuid had a little bit of land, and there was a fairy fort in the corner of one of his fields. Cooby liked to go into the fort to graze, but Diarmuid always drove her out, because it's well known that it's very bad luck to keep your animals in a fairy fort.

But when Diarmuid kept Cooby out of the fort, she pined away, and soon she wasn't giving the family any milk. Diarmuid was beside himself with worry – how was he going to feed his family? Then it got worse.

One morning, when he went out to his fields he found Cooby lying dead on the ground. The family was devastated – there would be no more good milk from Cooby and the children missed her.

A year later, soon after Diarmuid had left for the bog to cut some turf, his wife Deirdre was coming back through the fields with a basket of potatoes, when what did she see but a cow walking into the fairy fort, a cow that was the living image of Cooby. She had the same black spots on her back, the same bent horns.

Deirdre hid behind the hedge to watch, and when the cow came out of the fort again, there was a young girl with her, carrying a milking pail and stool. The girl sat down on the stool, put the pail under the cow and started milking.

Deirdre ran home as fast as she could to tell Diarmuid what she had seen.

'I could swear it was Cooby,' she said. 'She had the same spots and the bent horns and everything.'

'Well,' said Diarmuid, 'it's hard to believe that she's still alive. I buried her myself. But if it really is Cooby, I'll get her back and bring her home again, no matter who tries to stop me.'

'Be careful around the fort, Diarmuid,' said Deirdre. 'You don't want to cross the little people.'

Early the next morning Diarmuid left the house and walked across his land to the fairy fort. When he was not far away, he saw a white cow leaving the fort through the gap in the wall. He knew immediately that it was Cooby.

'Well, now,' he thought. 'Isn't that the strangest thing? My cow Cooby, that was dead, is walking around as large as life.'

Just then, a young girl with a milking stool and pail came out of the fort and set herself up beside the cow. Diarmuid ran up to the cow and took hold of one of her crooked horns. If he hadn't been convinced before, he certainly was now.

'Stop right now!' he shouted. 'Stop milking my cow!'

'Your cow?' said the astonished girl. 'Sure, this cow is ours the last year or more.'

'It's my cow that died a year ago. I'm sure of it, beyond the shadow of a doubt. Go to your master and tell him I want to speak with him.'

The girl got up from her stool and disappeared into the fort, taking her pail with her. When she came out again, there was a handsome young man with her.

'What are you doing here?' asked the young man. 'And why did you tell the girl to stop milking my cow?'

'It's not your cow, it's mine,' insisted Diarmuid. 'And I'll be taking her home with me right now!'

They argued and argued about whose cow it was, and all the while the shadows were getting longer and longer. Diarmuid knew that night would fall very soon and that Deirdre would be worried.

The young man turned on his heel and went back into the fort. Gathering up all his courage, Diarmuid went in after him. And there he saw an amazing sight – fairies and leprechauns dancing and laughing, and chubby little fairy children running around everywhere.

'You're a brave man to come into a fairy fort, Diarmuid,' the young man said. 'And because you're so brave, I'll tell you why we needed your cow – because it is, indeed, your good cow Cooby.'

'Why on earth would you need my cow?' asked Diarmuid, puzzled.

'Well,' said the young man, 'do you see all these children of ours running around? They needed milk and we had none to give them, and we knew that Cooby was the best milk cow for miles around.'

'She is a good milker, that's for sure,' agreed Diarmuid. 'But if you need her that badly, you can keep her. I wouldn't see little children go without milk.'

'Well,' smiled the young man, 'that's very kind of you, but our children are grown now and we have no more need of her. You can have her back,

and welcome. And from here on out, we'll help you whenever you need it and you'll grow rich and have good luck till the end of your days.'

So Diarmuid bid farewell to the fairies and he took the cow and drove her home. After that, Cooby had two calves every year and Diarmuid's mare had two foals every year and his sheep had two lambs every year and every acre of the land he had gave him as much crop in one year as another man could get from an acre in seven years. He was soon a very rich man; and why not, when the little people were on his side?

Lorcan and the Magic Purse

When Lorcan was a young lad, he loved listening to the amazing tales of fairies and leprechauns that his grandmother told him. He could have listened to them till the cows came home.

'You know,' said his grandmother, 'every leprechaun has a pot of gold, kept far away from the prying eyes of humans. They'll come up with every trick they can think of to stop us finding it, because if we do, they have to give it to us.'

'Oh, I'd love to get my hands on a pot of gold!' Lorcan was already thinking of ways of finding a leprechaun and tricking him into leading him to his hiding place.

'Of course,' continued his grandmother, 'once you find a leprechaun you must never let him out of your sight until you get the gold. If you can't get the pot of gold, you should try for his magic purse – it has only a shilling in it, but when you take the shilling out, another one appears in its place.'

From that day, Lorcan's only ambition was to trick a leprechaun into giving him his gold. He daydreamed his way through school, and his results weren't very good, so he couldn't find a job, even if he'd wanted to. No, Lorcan thought that he'd be a rich man – just as soon as he found that pot of fairy gold.

Soon, people were calling him Lazy Lorcan. He was never out of bed until long after the sun had risen, and he always looked half asleep, even in the middle of the day. When he was offered a day's work, he'd get there late and leave early. He was a pleasant chap, so he had lots of friends, but he never stood his round in the pub, probably because there was never anything in his wallet. Nobody really expected Lorcan to make anything of himself.

Lorcan had the idea that if he could just catch a leprechaun, he'd have no trouble making the little man give up the secret of his wealth. So he spent most of his days hidden behind the hedges all long the little lanes of the townland, listening out for the tap-tap-tapping of a leprechaun hard at work on his shoe repairs. Years went by – any normal person would have given up long ago, but Lorcan was sure he was going to make his fortune.

Sure enough, one day, just when Lorcan was about to set off home for his tea, what did he hear but a series of sharp taps. He crept towards the corner of the field they were coming from, keeping close to the hedge, and there, right in front of him, was the smallest man he had ever seen, sitting on a tree stump, hammering nails into a tiny shoe. Lorcan reached out and grabbed the little man round the neck.

'Hah! I've got you now!' he shouted triumphantly. 'Give me your gold, or I'll make sure you never see your family again!'

The leprechaun struggled and shouted and shrieked dreadfully, but no matter how much he wriggled and bellowed, Lorcan kept a firm grip.

'Give me your gold!' he shouted again, and he could feel that the leprechaun was getting tired.

'All right, so,' said the leprechaun. 'I'll bring you to the gold, but you'd better get yourself ready for a long journey, because I have it hidden in a safe place three valleys away from here.'

So off they went in the direction the leprechaun pointed out to Lorcan. They walked for hours, and hours … and hours. Lorcan was getting exhausted, and he was trying to keep his grip on the little man.

'Is it much further?' he asked.

'It is, so,' said the leprechaun. 'We probably won't get there for three days.'

'Three days!' Lorcan was beginning to feel very hungry (the leprechaun didn't seem to need any food, or rest) and, as we know, he was very lazy.

'I'd be quicker on my own, on my tiny fairy feet. I'd be back in half a day and I could leave you here to rest while I go off to get the gold for you,' offered the leprechaun innocently.

'Do you think I'm stupid?' growled Lorcan. 'I'm not letting you out of my sight.'

'Well,' said the leprechaun, 'what if I give you my purse for safekeeping? Look, here it is, with the magic shilling inside it. If I give you that, you can be sure I'll be back to claim it.'

'I suppose so,' said Lorcan, a bit doubtfully. 'Give me the purse, then I'll let go of you.'

So the leprechaun handed over the purse and Lorcan let him go. There was a puff of smoke, and the little man disappeared.

Lorcan waited for a full day, but there was no sign of the leprechaun. He realised that he'd been tricked.

'I should have known that would happen. But at least I have the magic purse, and I'll have enough shillings to last me the rest of my days.'

He went off home, and met up with his friends for a drink later that evening.

'Drink up, lads, drink up! The round's on me!' Never before had his friends heard the like of it.

'Are you sure you have money for this?' they asked.

'Sure, haven't I the magic purse?' boasted Lorcan, pulling it out for all to see.

'Open it, open it!' they called, because everyone would like to see a leprechaun's magic shilling at least once in their life.

So Lorcan opened the purse, laughing at his cleverness. Once the strings were loosened, everyone pushed through to see the magical coin that would make their friend rich. There was nothing in the purse only air. Lorcan shook the purse, pulling apart the lining and turning the little bag upside down, but eventually he had to admit that it was empty.

'That crafty leprechaun must have switched the purse when I wasn't looking. What a thing to do, to take advantage of a poor man like me.'

So his friends paid for the drinks, as usual, and the next day Lorcan was out hiding in the hedges again, waiting to come across another leprechaun. This time, he told himself, he was keeping a firm grip on him until he had the gold in his grasp.

49

Moving House

The Doyles were moving house! They'd finally decided that their cottage was too small for the whole family, especially now that the twins, Ruairí and Síle, needed separate rooms – Síle wanted a pink princess bedroom, while Ruairí wanted to sleep in a pirate ship. The best thing about the new house, though, was that there would also be a room just for Granny, who would be coming to live with them as soon as it was finished.

'It'll be great having Granny here all the time,' said Síle. 'She can tell us stories every day, not just when she comes to visit us.'

A plot of land had been bought, and plans for a large house were being drawn up.

Granny came to visit for a few days in the middle of all the planning and she, too, seemed excited about the new house.

'I'm so happy that you'll be coming to live with us, Granny,' said Síle. 'Isn't it great news about the house?'

'But where will you be building it?' Granny asked.

'In the top field, just past the cottage, where all the hawthorn bushes are,' said Ruairí. 'It's a great place – you can even see the sea from there.'

Granny looked worried.

'What's wrong, Granny?' asked Ruairí. 'Aren't you pleased about the new house?'

But Granny said nothing. She went to find the children's father, who was sorting out the final plans.

'Cathal,' she said, 'the children have just told me

where the new house is to be built. You can't possibly build it there – that spot with the hawthorn bushes is fairy ground.'

Cathal laughed. 'Don't be silly! Isn't that just one of the old tales? Nobody believes those any more! Anyway, they've been clearing the ground for days so that they can put in a solid foundation. Those old hawthorn roots go down for miles – they'd be bound to make the house unstable, so they all had to go.'

That really made Granny look worried, but she knew that her son had his mind made up and nothing she could say would change it.

The building work began a few weeks later and Ruairí and Síle rushed home from school every day to see how their new home was coming along. Every night the family gathered round the fire talking about how wonderful it would be when they moved into the new house, but whenever Granny was visiting, she was always very quiet during all these discussions, and she never seemed to be in the mood for telling stories.

Finally, the great day arrived when the family could move in to the new house. The twins had the day off school and had great fun organising their new bedrooms. Síle's was so beautiful that she really felt like a princess, and Ruairí was already dreaming of a life on the high seas. Their mother was delighted with her new kitchen, and Cathal was pleased that he'd decided to include a workshop in the plans.

All their neighbours and friends were invited to a grand housewarming party that night. It was a beautiful evening and people wandered in and out of the house, enjoying the warm night air. There was music and dancing and lots of food and drink.

At about midnight, the air began to cool and a breeze came up. People began to feel a bit chilly and they moved inside because the sky had clouded over and it looked as if it might start raining at any moment. No sooner was the front door shut behind them than a loud banging started up. It seemed to be coming from the roof.

'Now, that's strange,' said Cathal. 'I helped to put the roof on myself, and it was firmly nailed down. It couldn't possibly come loose in the first bit of wind it comes across.'

But the party atmosphere had vanished as soon as everyone had come inside, and people began to make their excuses and leave. When the last of them had departed for home, the banging noise seemed to spread to every bit of the house – it was coming from the walls, the floors and even the chimney.

'Granny was right all along!' cried the twins. 'The leprechauns and fairies want their land back!'

'You've really angered the little people,' said Granny. 'I tried to warn you, Cathal! We have to leave, now!

There's no time to waste if you want out get out of this house alive!'

The family rushed out of the juddering, shaking house. Cathal was the last to leave and he looked back at the house as he tried to shut the front door. He could see leprechauns banging and bashing at every part of the house in a fury. The door flew out of his hands, and then, with a great crash, the house fell down. The little people disappeared and all was quiet again.

The family moved back to their old cottage, their dreams of a new life in a new home completely shattered. All that remained of their fine new house was a pile of stones. Eventually even that disappeared under a new growth of hawthorn bushes, and from time to time the little people could be heard singing and dancing from the top of the hill.

Rainbow's End

One spring day when there was sunshine and rain in equal measure, Seamas O'Brien was walking along the road, wondering how the family would make ends meet. It had been a bad year for the farm and he was having to sell his cattle, one by one, to bring in some money. The rent was due and they wouldn't be able to pay it all, and he knew that the landlord would have no trouble kicking them all out onto the side of the road, children or no children.

He paused in the middle of the road to tie his bootlace, and glanced into the field to his right as he was getting up. He rubbed his eyes because he couldn't believe them – there it was, the end of a rainbow, right in the middle of Dinny Doyle's best pasture.

Seamas had heard of the end of the rainbow, but thought it was just a fairy tale, yet now, here it was, right in front of him. And, if he was right...yes! There it was, a glimmer of gold in the distance, just where the beautiful rainbow colours were bouncing off the grass.

Seamas sprinted into the field until he reached the little cauldron, which was filled to overflowing with gold coins. He plunged his hands deep into the treasure, loving the silky feel of the gold on his skin. He stayed there for several minutes, hardly believing his good luck, then he picked up the cauldron and ran home as fast as his legs could carry him.

Bursting through the front door, Seamas immediately called out to his wife, 'Oonagh! Oonagh! You will not believe what's just happened!'

Oonagh came out of the kitchen drying her hands –

she'd just been doing the washing up after dinner.

'Look what I found! Look what I found!' panted Seamas.

'Where in the world did you find that?' asked Oonagh. 'That looks like leprechaun gold.'

'I found it at the end of the rainbow in Dinny Doyle's top pasture,' said Seamas. 'I could hardly believe my eyes when I saw the gold glinting!'

'Well,' said Oonagh, 'If you found it in Dinny's

pasture, then it belongs to him, so you'll have to take it back again.'

'Take it back, woman? What are you thinking?' shouted Seamas. 'This is the best thing that's ever happened to us!'

'And it'll be the worst thing, if you don't take it back to its rightful owner, whether that owner is Dinny Doyle or a leprechaun.'

'I will not take it back,' said Seamas. 'If they're that careless with their treasure, they don't deserve to keep it. I'll go off down to the bank first thing in the morning to change some of these gold coins for notes.'

'Well, I'm having nothing to do with it,' retorted Oonagh. 'You're on your own. No good will come of this gold, I'm telling you.'

The next day, as soon as the bank had opened its doors, Seamas took in four of the coins to exchange them for cash.

'Where did you get these?' asked the bank manager, turning them over in his hands.

'I found them,' said Seamas. 'They belong to no one.'

'Well, they must belong to someone,' said Mr Dunphy. 'Where exactly did you find them?'

So Seamas told him the story of the rainbow.

'So it couldn't be Dinny's savings, you see. What fool would put his savings in a cauldron in the middle of a field and just leave them there?'

'But if they don't belong to Mr Doyle, then they're treasure and they belong to the government,' said Mr Dunphy. 'You can't keep that gold.'

'But you must have heard of the pot of gold at the end of a rainbow?' asked Seamas.

'I have, indeed,' agreed the bank manager.

'Well, I've just found it.'

'And you can't keep it. It belongs to the government.'

'No, that can't be right,' said Seamas angrily. He gathered up the coins and stormed out of the bank.

By the time he got home, he was very depressed.

'What good is this gold to me, Oonagh? I can't change it, so we can't spend it anywhere. I might as well not have found it in the first place.'

'Well, I did say no good would come of it,' said Oonagh, not unkindly. 'Why don't you have a nice cup of tea, then take it back where it came from and we'll forget all about it?'

So Seamas trudged gloomily back to Dinny Doyle's field and plonked the cauldron down in the spot where he'd found it. He was just walking away when he heard a voice coming from the direction of the wall.

'Haven't you forgotten something?'

Puzzled, Seamas stood there for a few moments and then, light dawned. He reached into his back pocket, pulled out the four coins he'd taken to the bank, and threw them in on top of the pile of gold. When he turned around, he saw that a leprechaun was sitting on the wall.

'Thank you, Seamas O'Brien,' he said. 'I thought I'd lost that for good. It wouldn't have been any good for you, you know. Leprechaun gold never works in the world of humans.'

And then he disappeared.

Seamas went home and – would you believe it? – from that day forward his life started to improve. He inherited a bigger and better farm and became prosperous, Oonagh grew wiser and more beautiful every day, and their children grew up strong and healthy and did well in life.

Seeing Red

Donal was walking along the road one day when he heard a strange noise coming from the field to his right. It wasn't harvest time yet, and the corn was still standing, so he knew that nobody could be working in the field. He looked through the hedge, and he saw a very strange sight – a little man, entirely dressed in green, with a big leather apron over his clothes. He was sitting on a stone with a brogue upside down in his lap, and he was levering off the heel of the shoe in order to repair it.

Now, Donal had heard stories of crocks of gold – it seemed that every leprechaun had one – and he thought that it would be a fine thing to get his hands on. He got close enough to the leprechaun to grab him if he had to, and then he said, 'Hello.'

'Well,' said the leprechaun, not looking very surprised, 'hello to you, too. What are you doing in my field at this time of the day?'

'Your field!' said Donal. 'Everyone knows this field belongs to Cormac O'Neill – it certainly isn't yours.'

'Is that so?' said the leprechaun. 'And who owns the one over there, then?' He was pointing his skinny little finger directly behind Donal.

Donal was just about to turn around to see which field the leprechaun was pointing at when he remembered, just in the nick of time, that if you take your eyes off a leprechaun, he'll disappear before he tells you where his crock of gold is.

'Hah!' he said, reaching out and grabbing the leprechaun by the collar of his coat. 'You don't fool me that easily, you wily little man. Now, will you tell me where your crock of gold is hidden?'

'If I do, will you leave me alone and let me get on with my work?' asked the leprechaun.

'I will, and gladly,' agreed Donal, certain that he'd be off spending all that lovely gold and would have no time to be pestering leprechauns.

'Well, it's a bit of a way, but I'll take you there, if you'll just put me down,' whined the little man.

'No, not till I've seen the gold,' said Donal, thinking that this was an easy way to get rich.

What he didn't realise is that it takes leprechauns a long time to gather together enough gold to fill a crock. They break into people's houses and shave tiny pieces off the edges of their gold coins, until they have enough gold to melt down and turn into new coins. If he had only known that, it would have been as plain a.

day to him that the leprechaun wasn't going to give up his treasure that easily.

Anyway, after a couple of hours' trekking over the fields, Donal holding the little man under his arm, they came to a cornfield, identical in every way to the one where Donal had come across the leprechaun.

'This is where my gold is,' said the leprechaun, waving towards the middle of the feld.

'You'll have to do better than that,' said Donal. 'I'll need to know where to dig.'

'What will you dig with?' asked the leprechaun. 'You don't have a spade with you.'

'Well, I'll just have to go back home to get one,' said Donal, 'and you'll have to come with me. I'm not letting you out of my sight.'

'If I tell you exactly where the gold is you could mark the spot with that nice red kerchief you have around your neck,' suggested the leprechaun. 'Then you can run off for your spade and dig up the gold when you get back, while I go off to finish my work. The gold is buried under this corn stalk,' he added, 'so why don't we tie the kerchief around it?'

Donal thought that it was bit odd that the leprechaun was being so helpful, but he couldn't see any flaw in the plan now that he knew where the gold was. He let go of the leprechaun, who ran off across the fields like greased lightning. With both hands finally free, Donal was able to tie his red kerchief to the cornstalk identified by the leprechaun.

He ran home as fast as he could and found his spade. He didn't even stop for a cup of tea, but raced back to the cornfield in case the leprechaun had changed his mind. He hoped it wouldn't take him too long to find the stalk with his red kerchief tied to it. The sight that met him as he approached the field made him think he was seeing things. He rubbed his eyes, but they hadn't been deceiving him – there was a red kerchief tied to every single stalk of corn in the enormous field.

Feeling both very foolish and very disappointed, Donal trudged home again, wondering if he'd ever have the good luck to come across a leprechaun again. If he did, he'd make sure to get his gold.

Taken for a Ride

Fiachra the farmer had a loyal dog called Bran, who went everywhere with him and slept outside at night to guard the house.

One day Fiachra noticed that Bran was very muddy and very tired and didn't have the energy to go around the farm with him that day.

'That's odd,' he thought. 'Bran is usually such a good companion. Perhaps he was out chasing rabbits last night and he just needs a rest.'

A few days later, Bran was in a bad state again and Fiachra was very puzzled.

'It's not like Bran to leave the farm at night,' he thought. 'Perhaps I should let him inside to sleep beside the stove.'

But Bran refused to come inside – his thick coat meant that he was uncomfortable in the well-heated farmhouse kitchen.

A week or so later, Fiachra whistled for Bran, but the dog was too tired to move and was covered in dried mud again.

'Right!' thought Fiachra. 'There's something odd about this, so I'm staying up tonight to see if I can find out what's going on.'

That night, Fiachra hid himself in the barn and waited to see what would happen. The sun rose the next morning and Bran hadn't left his kennel all night. Fiachra did the same thing the next night, determined to get to the bottom of the problem. Again, Bran stayed in his kennel all night long. Then, on the third night, at about midnight, Fiachra heard scuffles coming from the yard and the sound of a harness being put on a horse. What could be happening?

He crept out and saw the strangest sight! There was a leprechaun sitting on Bran, on a little tooled leather saddle, a fine crop trimmed with gold in his hand.

'Hup!' said the leprechaun, and off they went, Bran running across the countryside like a prize racehorse, with the leprechaun hanging on to the saddle. They had disappeared from sight before Fiachra could even saddle his horse. He waited in the yard and, just before sunrise, Bran slunk back, covered in mud, panting.

Fiachra kept up his vigil for a few more nights, making sure his horse was saddled up and ready to go. Sure enough, the leprechaun appeared again, and as soon as he'd ridden away on Bran, Fiachra mounted his horse and followed them.

Eventually, he saw Bran lying under a bush, resting, and he could see light a little further on. He tethered his horse to a tree and crept forward on foot, closer and closer to the light. As he approached, he could hear music and merriment. When he got to the bush where Bran was resting, he parted the leaves and saw a whole gathering of fairies and leprechauns, dancing and making merry. He stayed watching for a while, then he went back to his horse and rode home.

A few nights later he lay in wait for the leprechaun, just behind Bran's kennel. Sure enough, along came the leprechaun with his saddle and crop. He was just saddling up the poor dog when Fiachra jumped out and grabbed the little man.

'Why are you stealing my dog?' he asked.

'Sure, I'm not stealing him, only borrowing him. I

eed a good mount to take me to the gatherings of our
people and I have no horse.'

'Well, you've worn him out to the point where he's
no good to me,' said Fiachra angrily, 'and now you're
in debt to me!'

'What do you want?' asked the little man. 'Not the
gold, I hope – another human had that off me a year
since, and I've only one gold coin to my name.'

'No, no, not the gold,' said Fiachra, impatiently.
'I have no need of more money. But I do need a good
servant, so you'll have to serve me for a year and a day
to repay the debt.'

The leprechaun thought about it and realised he'd
have a year of good food and lodging, so he agreed.

As it turned out, the leprechaun was an excellent
servant and a great cook. Never had the family eaten
so well!

Well, the year and a day came to an end soon enough. Fiachra's wife Fionnuala wanted him to make the leprechaun stay.

'A deal's a deal,' said Fiachra. 'You can't expect me to go back on my word.'

Just as the leprechaun was about to set off for his own world again, Fiachra stopped him.

'I have a gift for you,' he said, leading the leprechaun to the side of the barn. There stood a beautiful Connemara pony, fitted out with a fine leather saddle and bridle.

'This is for you,' said Fiachra to the astonished leprechaun. 'You'll still need a mount to get you to the gatherings of your people.'

'You're a good man, Fiachra,' said the leprechaun. 'May every blessing come your way.'

82

Off he galloped, and that was the last that Fiachra (or Bran) ever saw of him.

And the interesting thing is that Fiachra's farm prospered from that day forward, even when other farms were having hard times, Fionnuala found a fine cook for their kitchen, and Bran ... well, Bran lived out the rest of his days in comfort and peace, with no midnight excursions to tire him out.

The Dream

Eoin O'Shaughnessy was a travelling tailor in the days when people would have the tailor in for a week to sew their clothes for the coming year.

One time, he had just arrived at the home of the Rooney family and was sitting at the big kitchen table, sewing a suit and chatting to the woman of the house about this and that and the other thing.

All at once, he leaned forward and said, in a hushed voice, 'Would you believe me, Mrs Rooney, if I told you I had a dream about a crock of gold buried under a tree not far from this place?'

'I would, Mr O'Shaugnessy,' she replied. 'Many a man has a dream about a crock of gold, but none I know has ever found one.'

'No, no!' he said adamantly. 'This dream was as clear as the day. The crock was buried under the crooked hawthorn tree at the bottom of Caomhín Burke's big pasture, not two miles from here.'

'Is that so?' asked Mrs Rooney, thinking that she'd never before heard of a dream that was so clear and gave the dreamer so much detail.

'Actually,' said the tailor, 'I can't just sit here while I know that all that gold is just waiting for me to dig it up. What if someone else has had the same dream and gets there before me? Oh, but I have no shovel.'

'Well now, Mr O'Shaugnessy, I can lend you one and gladly. My Billy keeps one in that bothán just beside the back gate. You can collect it as you leave.'

So off the tailor went, sure that he was about to make his fortune. He walked the two miles to the crooked hawthorn tree, and circled it until he was sure he had the right spot, as shown to him in his dream. Then he started digging, and he dug, and dug and dug

The next thing he knew he was waking up in the little bed that he used whenever he was tailoring for th Rooneys. And there was Mrs Rooney, with a soothing drink for him.

'What happened?' he groaned, rubbing the lump on his aching head.

'Well,' said Mrs Rooney, 'It was the strangest thing. Off you went two days ago with your shovel over your shoulder, all set to dig up the crock of gold that you'd seen in your dream. The next thing I knew, you were back, raving about leprechauns, with your hands all torn and blistered. So I bandaged your hands and put you to bed.'

'And did I have anything with me?' asked the tailor, in desperation.

'Apart from the shovel and a lot of mud sticking to your boots, not a thing,' said Mrs Rooney, not quite meeting his eye, but the tailor was so upset he didn't notice that she was behaving a bit oddly.

'I could have sworn I'd found the crock of gold, and had just heaved it out of the hole in the ground when a leprechaun appeared out of nowhere and tried to take it away from me.'

'Ah well, he must have succeeded, so,' said Mrs Rooney, 'for you were empty-handed when you arrived back at the house.'

'No, no, that can't be right,' said the tailor. 'I'm going back up to the crooked hawthorn tree. I have such a clear memory of pulling the crock of gold out from under it.'

So off he went, but the story had spread and this time there was a crowd of onlookers. When they got to the hawthorn tree, there, sure enough, was an enormous hole, so big that the tree was sagging into it.

'There, do you see?' asked the tailor. 'I definitely got the crock of gold out from under that tree. It's all coming back to me.'

'But, sure,' interrupted Mrs Rooney, 'didn't you say you had a huge struggle with the leprechaun who owned the gold? He must have taken it from you and moved it to a new hiding place. Come back to the house with me now and have a nice cup of tea.'

Mr O'Shaughnessy scratched his head, puzzled and disappointed.

'Aye, that must be it,' he said. 'And I suppose I'll never get a chance like that again.'

It was often remarked in the locality afterwards how prosperous the Rooneys had got lately; they had never been poor, but now they never seemed to be short of money. And, to be fair, Mrs Rooney always welcomed the tailor and gave him the best of food and lodging whenever he came to her house on his rounds.

The Fairy Cloak

Niall was a hardworking young farmer, with just one problem – he didn't have enough land to work. His little farm was on a spit of land that was surrounded on three sides by the sea, so he knew that he couldn't expect to find any more land in that direction. His neighbour on the fourth side refused to sell to him, even though he wasn't farming his land – he just liked owning it. But if Niall was going to make a decent living, he needed more land!

When he was a child, he'd often crept out of bed at night and hidden at the top of the stairs, listening avidly to the adults sitting around the fire, telling tales of fairies, leprechauns and ghosts. Now that he was grown up, he found the stories hard to believe (he'd never actually seen one of the little people), but there was one story that stuck in his mind because it gave him some hope for a solution to his problem.

It was said that once every seven years the tide went right out, out as far as the horizon. When that happened, the little people arrived for a party. They had a big blanket that they spread out on the sand, and this blanket was able to keep the tide back, so that the sea wouldn't come in to spoil their fun. Not only that, any land that was held back by the blanket in this way was magically turned into good farming land, where you could grow anything at all that you wanted, as long as you were in possession of the blanket.

Niall thought that there must be some way that he could make use of this strange event. When he was still a child, he'd crept out of the house on the night of the little people's party and hidden behind the big rocks at the edge of the beach.

Sure enough, the tide rolled right out, out as far as the eye could see, and along came a big crowd of little people, leprechauns and fairies and sprites. One of the leprechauns reached into his leather purse and pulled out a small piece of folded cloth. He shook it out and it spread out and out until it covered a large bit of the dry land. Then a group of leprechauns sat on the blanket, got out their cobbling tools and began to hammer at the tiny shoes they had brought with them.

A couple of leprechauns were playing their fiddles while the others worked, and the fairies and sprites were dancing. As long as the leprechauns sat there the tide stayed out, and all the while the grass was growing, so that by the time they stood up, folded up the blanket and disappeared, the whole beach looked like good pasture land – until the tide came in again and swallowed it up.

Tonight was the night of the little people's party and Niall had decided that he'd get his hands on that blanket, by hook or by crook. He muffled his horse's hooves with bits of sacking and rode in the direction of the shore. He tethered the horse close to the spot where he had hidden seven years earlier.

As he approached the rocks, he could hear the fairy music, wafting towards him on the breeze. He got closer and there they were again, the little group of leprechauns, sitting on their magic blanket and repairing their tiny shoes, tapping away in time to the lilting music.

There was a strong breeze that night, and Niall could see that the four corners of the blanket were flapping. He thought that if he could just get hold of one corner, he could pull the blanket out from under the leprechauns. He moved forward carefully, keeping to the shadows, but no matter how far he went, he still seemed to have the same distance to go, and the shoreline was getting further and further away.

Finally, he reached the edge of the blanket. Crouching down, he put his hand out and took hold of a corner with a firm grasp. Gritting his teeth, he tugged at the blanket and … it worked! He had pulled the blanket out from under the leprechauns. Then, without warning, everything was plunged into complete darkness, and he could hear the leprechauns shouting as he raced off in the direction of his horse, the magic blanket in his hand.

Suddenly all the noise and confusion stopped and it became very quiet.

'That's that, then,' thought Niall. 'I've done it! I've got the blanket and the leprechauns have disappeared.'

He climbed on his horse, tucking the blanket (which was as fine as gossamer) in his pocket, and he galloped in the direction of his farmhouse. As he rode, he thought he could hear a faint rumbling sound, which got louder ... and louder ... and LOUDER! He turned around and what did he see but an enormous wave, heading towards him. He spurred his horse, galloping as fast as he could to keep ahead of it. Suddenly, he was swept off the horse and he felt lots of little hands beating him and pulling at him.

Then, as suddenly as it had appeared, the wave disappeared and Niall was left lying on the ground, exhausted. He fell into a deep sleep and woke up feeling as sore and stiff as if he'd just fought in a battle.

'Thank goodness I survived that,' he thought. 'And at least I still have the fairy blanket, safe and sound, so I'll soon have all the land I need.' He could feel the blanket in his pocket and he reached in to pull it out. Imagine his surprise when all he found was a handful of wet, slimy seaweed.

And that was the last time anyone managed to get their hands on the fairy blanket. If you go down to the shore every seven years on the appointed day, you'll find the leprechauns sitting on their blanket, chatting and singing and tapping away at their shoes, and if you look very closely, you'll see that the corners of the blanket are tied to the ground with four magic tent pegs.

The Fairy Fort

Orla and her brother Feargal lived very near a lios, a fairy fort. In summer, the fort was covered with beautiful wild flowers, but Orla's mother always warned her not to pick them.

'It's bad luck,' she said. 'If you pick their flowers, the little people will be angry. They're happy to share them with us when they're out in the open, in the fresh air, but they don't like us to bring their flowers inside the house.'

But one beautiful sunny day, when Orla and Feargal were out in the field picking flowers for the house, Orla forgot her mother's warning and moved closer and closer to the fairy fort, where there seemed to be more bees and butterflies flying around.

'Don't go too close to the fort, Orla,' called Feargal, when he saw how far away she was. 'You know those flowers will bring you nothing but bad luck.'

But the flowers there were so beautiful that Orla couldn't resist picking them.

'There are so many flowers here I'm sure they won't miss a few,' she thought. 'And they'll look so lovely on the kitchen table.'

Orla and Feargal were home in time for lunch and their mother put the lovely flowers on the kitchen table in a jam jar.

'Where did you find such lovely flowers?' she asked.

'Orla picked them in the fairy fort,' admitted Feargal. 'I told her not to, but she didn't take any notice of me.'

As soon as their mother heard that the flowers had come from the fairy fort, she rushed outside with them and put them on the window ledge. She hoped the fairies hadn't noticed that they'd been inside for half an hour, because she knew that they'd be looking for revenge if they did.

That night, Orla went to bed as usual, but as soon as she got in, she hopped out again, screaming. Her bed was full of stinging nettles and they seemed to be growing by the minute! She got into her parents' bed, but the same thing happened, and in the bed in the guest room. There wasn't a bed in the house that she could sleep in. Every time she pulled back the covers to climb in, the nettles started growing again. After three sleepless nights, the whole family was feeling desperate.

'I knew no good would come of taking flowers from the lios!' cried her mother. 'What are we going to do?'

Orla's father had heard about a wise woman who lived nearby, so they visited her and asked her what they should do.

'It won't be easy to please the fairies,' she said. 'They get very upset if anyone interferes with what belongs to them. But if you could do a good deed for them, they might have pity on your daughter.'

The family put their heads together to come up with some good deed that they could do for the fairies, but they couldn't think of anything. What could they possibly do for the little people that they couldn't do for themselves? They thought and thought, but nothing came into their minds.

Finally, Feargal had an idea. Without saying anything to anyone he crept out of the house in the middle of the night and went to the fairy fort. At midnight, the lights started twinkling in the fort and lovely music started playing. Feargal knew that the fairies loved music and he played a few instruments himself, including the feadóg.

Feargal edged forward, parting the bushes when he got close to the light, and an amazing sight met his eyes! There was any number of fairies and leprechauns having a céilidh. There were leprechauns standing around the edge of the clearing playing fiddles and feadógs. 'Hey!' thought Feargal, 'their feadógs are just like mine, only much smaller.'

As soon as the music stopped, Feargal stepped into the light. Silence fell – you could have heard a pin drop. One of the leprechauns stepped forward.

'Your sister trespassed on our fort and now you're disturbing our dancing,' he said angrily.

'No,' said Feargal, 'that's not it at all. I came to tell you that Orla's sorry, really sorry, and will never do such a thing again. She hasn't had any sleep in a week – please take the nettles out of her bed!'

'Certainly not,' replied the leprechaun. 'If we do that, the next thing we know, everyone will be stealing from us.' He turned his back on Feargal and ordered the musicians to start the music up again.

Feargal wasn't sure what to do. It seemed that he'd reached the end of the road and that poor Orla would be sleeping on a bed of nettles for the rest of her days. When the music stopped again, he decided to make one last attempt. He stepped into the centre of the clearing, took his feadóg out of his pocket, and began to play a slow, sad tune. The little people stopped talking and moving around and began to listen, enchanted by the lovely music.

When Feargal stopped playing, there was complete silence for a couple of seconds, and then the fairies and leprechauns started clapping.

'Well done, Feargal!' they called. 'What a lovely tune. Would you give it to us?'

'I would, of course,' said Feargal, 'and I have a few more, too, that I could play for you now.'

'Well,' said the leprechauns when he had finished playing, 'we'll have to reward you for bringing us all this lovely music.'

'Oh, I don't need a reward. I just want you to help Orla.'

'All right, so,' they said. 'We agree. If you go home now, you'll find your sister sleeping peacefully.'

Dawn was breaking as Feargal left the fort. He

urned around to wave goodbye to
he little people, but the place was
completely empty!

As soon as he got home, he went
o Orla's bedroom and found her fast
sleep in bed. Everyone was delighted
 they knew that Feargal had had
omething to do with the lifting of
he spell, but he never told them what
ad happened that night in the fairy
ort. And Orla never went within
wenty paces of the fort again.

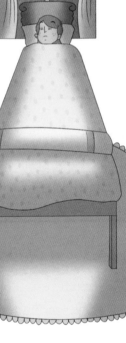

The Haunted Cellar

The Burke family of Athenry in County Galway was well known for its hospitality and the size of its wine cellar. Many a good evening's entertainment was enjoyed in the Burke home by the families of the area. Whenever the wine on the table was getting low, James Burke would send his butler down to the cellar to get a few more bottles.

But there was a problem, a big problem. No sooner had a butler been trained into his master's ways and the geography of the house than he would start being unreliable and then, as sure as anything, he would up and leave, sometimes without even giving notice. James Burke was at his wit's end trying to find a butler who would stay in his service for more than few months. He paid more than any master in the county and had better servants' quarters than any other house in the province, but nothing seemed to make any difference. It all seemed to start when he brought a new man on a tour of the cellar.

Well, all this while there was a young lad working in the stables, and he'd seen quite a few butlers come and go. He was very keen to better himself in life and had no intention of being a stable boy for ever.

'I could do that job, easy,' thought Pádraig (for that was his name), but he couldn't think of a way to bring himself to the attention of the master.

One market day the master's lawyer arrived, and because everyone had gone to the market, there was no one to show him to the master's library.

Pádraig brought the man inside.

'Come in, come in, and welcome,' said the master.

'Can I offer you a nice glass of hock? Oh no, I can't, because my butler has just left and I have no wine upstairs. You, boy,' he said, suddenly noticing Pádraig standing in the doorway. 'Could you find your way down into the cellar and bring up two of the bottles in the green crate nearest the entrance?'

'I could, your honour,' said the boy, thrilled to be given this chance.

'Get a lantern in the kitchen, so,' said Burke. 'It's very dark down there.'

So Pádraig went to the kitchen and found a lantern. He lit it, even though it was still broad daylight, and opened the door to the cellar. When he had gone down a few steps, the darkness surrounded him and it was so cold he started shivering. The light of the lantern was hardly strong enough to pierce the gloom, but he

116

eventually picked out the green crate in the dim glow, grabbed two bottles and ran up the stairs with them.

Of course, James Burke was delighted.

'How you would you like to be my butler, boy?' he asked, kindly.

Pádraig was beginning to understand why so many butlers had left after such a short time in the master's service, but he knew he couldn't give up this chance.

'I would, sir, and gladly,' he agreed.

Well, everything went well for quite a long time. Pádraig always went down to the cellar during the day, and he wedged open the cellar door with a bit of wood so that it couldn't slam behind him in the wind. All went well until one night, when there was a big feast at the house. Although Pádraig had brought up several cases of wine that day, the guests were thirsty and the bottles ran dry. Pádraig was summoned and told to go down into the cellar and get a dozen more bottles.

Summoning up all his courage, the boy took a lantern and opened the cellar door, wedging it open with his bit of wood. Halfway down the stairs he heard the door slam shut and the flame in his lamp blew out. Then he heard strange laughter, getting closer, and closer … he dashed up the stairs and burst through the cellar door into the light. When Burke got tired of waiting for his wine he came looking for Pádraig and found the lad slumped against the wall, his eyes glazed and unfocused.

'What the …!' he shouted. 'Am I not to be master in my own house and have wine when I need it?'

He went back to his guests to explain the reason for their thirst.

'I'll just have to sell this house and move somewhere else,' he said. 'But in the meantime, I'm off to the cellar to get some more wine for you.'

Grabbing another lantern, he stormed down the cellar stairs – and there, sitting on top of one of the crates, was the ugliest little man you've ever seen.

'You!' Burke shouted. 'I thought we'd got rid of you ten years ago. No wonder all my servants are terrified.'

'Well,' whined the little man, 'it's warm and comfortable here, and there's plenty to drink, so I came back. You'd need to have a very good bribe to make me leave again.'

'Bribe, is it?' shouted Burke. 'I'm leaving this place, and I'll be taking the wine with me!'

'Right you are,' said the leprechaun (for that is who he was, and not one of the friendly ones either). 'I'll be

coming with you, for I'm linked to your life from here on out.'

'Well,' said Burke, 'if that's the way of it, I'm not moving. Stay in this cellar for as long as you like. You don't frighten me.'

And from that day, James Burke always fetched the wine from the cellar himself, but he never bought any more, so that by the time he died the cellar was empty, and the haunting by the leprechaun was brought to an end, he having no reason to continue it.

Burke's son and heir, and his son's sons and heirs, all had the pleasure of living in that fine house, although they were all teetotallers, every one of them.

The Leprechaun's Honey

It's well known that the little people love honey – it's one of the reasons their fairy forts have so many beautiful flowers growing in them. The little people grow them for the bees so that the bees can make honey, and the bees are always happy to give them some.

One particular leprechaun was so fond of honey that he always put by a big store of a dozen large jars to see him through the winter. He built it up by growing beautifully scented flowers for the bees and by being so pleasant to them that they gave up their honeycombs willingly. He wasn't too keen on sharing it with anyone else, especially visitors who told him that he'd never be able to eat it all himself – he knew what they were thinking, and he certainly wasn't going to let them get their hands on it. His friend Fox was

particularly fond of honey himself, but he was also far too lazy to make friends with the bees.

Every day, the leprechaun went out for a long walk. One day when he came back he thought he'd have a nice meal of toast and honey, but when he went to his larder, there were only eleven jars of honey.

'That's strange,' he thought. 'I could have sworn I had a dozen jars in the larder – but perhaps I just didn't count them properly.'

The next day he went off for his walk, and when he came back there were only ten jars. He knew he hadn't miscounted again, and when Fox called round, he told him what had happened.

'That's very odd,' said Fox. 'Who do you know who loves honey as much as you do?'

'Well,' said the leprechaun, 'that's the thing. I know

lots of people who love honey …' and he suddenly realised that he was looking at one of them. He knew that he'd have to come up with a clever plan to catch the honey thief.

The next day, the leprechaun decided to visit his friend Little Pig.

'Well,' said Little Pig, when he saw who had knocked on his door. 'Isn't this a pleasant surprise!' He invited the leprechaun to warm himself by the fire.

'You look worried, my friend,' he said.

'I am worried,' said the leprechaun. 'The thing is, someone has been stealing my honey. I wanted to ask you if you'd hide yourself near my house when I go out for my walk and see who the thief is.'

'Stealing your honey?' said Little Pig, who was quite fond of honey himself. 'That's a shameful thing to do.'

'Well, yes, it is,' said the leprechaun, 'I'm so keen to find the thief that I'll give half my store to whoever discovers who it is.'

That was enough to put a seal on the bargain and the next day, when the leprechaun went out for his walk, Little Pig hid himself behind a bush next to the leprechaun's front door. Soon enough, who did he see coming along the road only Fox, the leprechaun's good friend, looking around him to see that no one was following him.

'He's definitely after the leprechaun's honey,' thought Little Pig, as Fox disappeared through an open side window in the leprechaun's house.

Sure enough, out came Fox a few minutes later, carrying a big jar of honey. So now Little Pig knew who the thief was.

By the time the leprechaun got home, Little Pig was jumping up and down with excitement.

'I know who the thief is, I know who the thief is!' he cried triumphantly.

'Well,' said the leprechaun, 'I had a good idea that it was Fox, but I had no proof. Why don't we go inside and have some tea and honey, and I'll decide what to do about him?'

Little Pig and the leprechaun had a delicious meal of toast and honey, and by the time they'd finished eating the leprechaun had thought of a way to stop Fox stealing his honey.

'I'll just need to talk to some friends of mine,' he said to Little Pig. 'Why don't you come along tomorrow afternoon and we'll see if my plan works?'

Little Pig had no idea how the leprechaun was going to save his honey, but he knew that he was a very clever chap and that most of his plans worked out well.

The next day, the leprechaun went out for his walk, as usual, leaving Little Pig hiding behind the bush again. Along came Fox, just as he had the day before, and he climbed through the little window again. Out he came, carrying a jar of honey, and was about to go back the way he came when Little Pig accidentally stepped on a twig. The loud crack startled Fox, who looked at the bush very suspiciously, and he started to move forward to investigate. Little Pig was shaking in his boots.

'Only me,' said Rabbit, stepping out from under the bush. 'I was just on my way to visit the leprechaun.'

'Well, he's not in at the moment,' said Fox. 'I can't wait around any longer, hoping that he'll turn up. I had a nice jar of honey to give him, because I know he loves honey.' And off he went down the road, clutching his jar of honey.

Little Pig almost exploded with anger when he heard Fox's lies.

'I hope the leprechaun's plan works,' he said to himself. 'Otherwise that thief will soon make off with ALL his honey!'

Just then, he heard a low rumbling in the distance, a noise that got louder … and louder … and LOUDER! He turned to look behind him and saw a huge swarm of bees flying in the direction that Fox had taken. After a

132

few moments he heard a terrible shrieking, and then he saw a red flash streaking across the fields.

After a few minutes, the leprechaun came along, whistling a happy tune and carrying the stolen jar of honey under his arm.

'That fixed him,' he said to the astonished Little Pig and Rabbit (who had stayed around to watch the fun). 'I told the bees he was stealing their hard-earned honey and they were very angry. I don't think we'll be seeing him around here again.'

And they all went inside for a nice cup of tea. The leprechaun was as good as his word and when Little Pig left for home, he was pulling a small cart that had five large jars of honey safely stacked inside.

The Long Dance

Once upon a time there was a girl called Eithne, and there was nothing that she liked more than music and dancing. It was all her mother could do to get her to go to school and finish her homework. Eithne's older brother, Mícheál, had to walk her to school and back home again; otherwise she'd be off in the fields, looking for fairies, who she had heard were great dancers.

One night, Eithne was fast asleep, dreaming that she was at a fairy ball, when she was woken by a strange sound. She'd heard it before, but this time she decided that she would find out what it was.

She crept downstairs, opened the back door of the house and stepped outside. She was lucky that there was a full moon that night, which meant everything was brightly lit. She heard a movement behind her, turned around, and there was her big brother.

'What are you doing outside on your own in the middle of the night?' he asked crossly.

'I heard that noise again – it sounds like some kind of music – and I'm going to find out what's going on. You can't stop me.'

'Well, I'm coming with you, then,' said Mícheál, because he knew his parents would expect him to look after his little sister. He was quite excited at the prospect of an adventure, although he didn't let on to Eithne that he was happy at the prospect of wandering around the countryside in the middle of the night.

'Where was the music coming from?' asked Mícheál.

'I'm not sure,' said Eithne. 'Shush, and listen for a bit.'

So the two children stood stock still in the silver moonlight and listened. They could hear leaves rustling and an owl hooting in the distance, but no music reached their ears.

'I think it's the fairy people,' said Eithne, who had always loved listening to her grandmother's stories of the little people.

'Don't be silly,' said Mícheál. 'There's no such thing as fairies.'

'There are so fairies,' said Eithne. 'Anyway, if you don't want to come, don't, but I'm off to see if I can find them.'

Mícheál didn't want to let her go off on her own, so he took her hand, and off they went into the woods. As they got closer to the middle, they began to see

flickering lights and then they heard music – lovely light, tinkling music. Eithne was entranced.

'I think the music is calling me,' she said, and she moved closer to the clearing where the music seemed to be coming from.

'Don't get too close,' warned Mícheál. 'Granny said the little people steal children.'

'I thought you said you didn't believe in them,' scoffed Eithne.

'Well, I don't … not really, but just to be on the safe side …'

But Eithne had parted the leaves and had found something astonishing.

'Look', she said excitedly. 'Look, there they are. I just knew I was hearing fairy music!'

Mícheál crawled up behind her and he couldn't believe what he was seeing, even though it was right in front his eyes. Tiny sparkling lights were hanging from the branches and there was a whole gathering of little people dancing in the clearing to the lovely lilting music played by leprechauns on feadógs, fiddles and a harp.

The music changed tempo suddenly, getting faster and faster, and soon the dancers were whirling around the clearing.

Eithne felt herself being drawn in to the dance and she moved forward. Too late, Mícheál remembered that his grandmother had said that if you ever heard the fairy music, you should cover your ears.

Soon Eithne had moved into the middle of the dancers and was moving in time with the music.

Mícheál had covered his ears and was trying to think of some way to get Eithne's attention, but he couldn't even wave at her without uncovering his ears. Suddenly there was a blinding flash and Mícheál felt himself falling. He landed with a bump on the grass, and when he looked around him, he was completely alone. Everyone, the fairies, the leprechauns and, most importantly, his sister had all vanished.

People searched for Eithne for years, but nobody ever found the slightest trace of her. It was as if she'd never existed. Mícheál grew up and moved to a different part of the country, but he never forgot his little sister. Whenever he visited his parents, he went to the clearing in the woods where he had last seen her.

One day, he was walking through the woods when he heard a little voice calling, 'Mícheál, Mícheál! Where are you? The dancing is finished and I want to go home!'

He turned around, and there on the path was Eithne. She hadn't aged a day in all the time she'd been missing and she looked looked just like the little girl who had disappeared that night all those years ago.

'Have you seen my big brother?' she asked him. 'I was dancing with the fairies and leprechauns for twenty minutes and he must have wandered off. Now I can't find him and it's time for us to go home.'

Mícheál looked at her, astonished.

'Is it really you, Eithne? I'm your brother, Mícheál!'

'Don't be silly,' scoffed the little girl. 'My brother is a young boy, not a man.'

'But you've been away dancing for twenty years, not twenty minutes,' said Mícheál. 'We've been looking for you all that time.'

They went home to a great reunion – and every day for the next twenty days, Eithne gained a whole year, until she was a beautiful young woman. She lived a long and happy life and she never forgot her adventure with the little people, although she never danced with them again.

The Lost Children

Seán and Sinéad were very young when their mother died, and they didn't really remember her. After a few years, their father married again, a fine strong woman who was distantly related to the fairy people. She wasn't very fond of the children, and she made them work hard from dawn to dusk. Their father didn't know how a good mother should behave, and as long as the children were healthy and well fed, he didn't raise any objections.

One day, Seán and Sinéad were out in the woods near their home, gathering small bits of wood to be used as kindling for the fire. The basket was beginning to get very heavy, and they knew they wouldn't be able to carry much more. They were just about to set off home again when, suddenly, they came upon a little man, dressed in a red coat and green britches, with shiny buckles on his black boots, standing in front of them on the path.

'What are your names, children?' he asked kindly.

'I'm Seán, and this is my little sister, Sinéad,' replied Seán politely, because the children were not only obedient, but had very good manners.

'And what are you up to today?' asked the little man. 'Did you come into the woods to play games?'

'We don't know what games are,' replied Sinéad. 'We came into the woods to gather some firewood for our stepmother, and now we have to be getting back home with it.'

'Right so,' said the little man. 'You go off home, and I'll see you again the next time you come this way.'

The children went home, talking all the way about the strange little man.

'Who do you think he is?' asked Sinéad.

'I think he might be a leprechaun,' replied Seán. 'I heard our father and stepmother talking about them one night when they thought I was asleep.'

'But I thought leprechauns were bad,' said Sinéad. 'That one seemed very friendly and nice.'

'Well, let's hope we see him again,' said Seán.

A few weeks later, the children were gathering mushrooms for supper at the edge of the wood when, suddenly, there he was again, the friendly leprechaun. The children were delighted.

'I'm glad to see you again,' he said, 'because I thought I could teach you a few games. You said you didn't know what they are,' he went on, smiling at the two children. 'I know a great one called leapfrog – I can teach you how to play it, if you like.'

'Oh, yes, please,' chorused the children. 'We'd love to learn a game!'

'Well,' said the leprechaun, 'here's what you must do. You bend down here, Sinéad, and Seán leaps over your back, then he bends down where he lands, and I leap over you, and then over Seán, and then I bend down and it's your turn to leap over the pair of us. It sounds more complicated than it is.'

So they all started leapfrogging towards the woods. The children were having so much fun that they didn't notice how deep into the woods they were travelling. They went as far as the outer edge of the woods and leapfrogged right up to a crooked hawthorn tree in the middle of a field. The leprechaun bent down very close to the roots of the tree. Seán leapfrogged over him and slid down the roots, disappearing underneath the tree. Then Sinéad did the same thing.

The leprechaun snapped his fingers, rubbed one leg against the other, and then he jumped under the tree after them.

When the children disappeared under the tree, they slid down a narrow tunnel that dropped them, standing, in a little room that had been hollowed out beneath the tree in such a way that the roots were taking the place of furniture.

It was very dark in this strange room under the tree and it took a while for Seán and Sinéad's eyes to get used to the lack of light. When they did, they saw six little men dressed in green, with long leather

aprons over their clothes, sitting in a circle making and repairing shoes.

As soon as Seán realised that he was in a room, he took off his cap and bowed, and Sinéad dropped a little curtsey, for, as we have seen, these children were very well-mannered.

The leprechaun who had brought them there sat the pair of them on a large root.

'Make yourselves comfortable there,' he said, 'and I'll measure you both for a pair of shoes, the best shoes you'll ever have.'

'Is that what you do all day?' asked Seán. 'Make shoes?'

'Indeed it is, unless we have to make clothes for ourselves, but we prefer to make shoes, because that's proper work for a leprechaun. Sometimes we have to squeeze ourselves through the gaps in the windows of human houses to shave bits of gold off the coins. We need to have a crock of gold at the ready in case we get caught by a human and we have to ransom ourselves.'

'Does that happen often?' asked Sinéad, wide-eyed.

'Indeed and it does not,' declared the leprechaun, 'because we're wilier than most humans.'

Now, while the shoes were being made for the children, their stepmother had realised that they were very late coming home. She knew her husband would blame her if the children were missing, so she went out to look for them. Because she had fairy blood herself, soon she found a trail that led to the hawthorn tree. She called the leprechaun out.

'Where are those children?' she demanded angrily.

'Those children who didn't know how to play a game?' asked the leprechaun. 'We're looking after them, better than you ever did.'

'Give them back at once!' she shrieked.

'Well, if you make yourself small enough, you can come down and get them yourself,' offered the leprechaun, smirking.

'I will not,' she retorted. 'I don't have the magic to make myself big again, and well you know it.'

'Well, then,' said the leprechaun. 'You have a bit of a problem.'

'If you don't let those children go, I'll bring the fairies of Glencar here. They're my kin, and you'll remember what happened when the leprechauns stole the child of the Queen of the Fairies,' she threatened.

The leprechaun remembered only too well, and he knew that he couldn't get into a battle like that again.

'All right, so,' he said. 'I'll bring them up – on condition that you look after them better and give them some playtime every day. Otherwise, I'll see to it that their father gets to hear about the way you treat them like servants.'

The stepmother knew she was getting the best of the bargain – she could still get some work out of the children, even if they had some playtime – so she agreed to his conditions.

The leprechaun led the children, wearing their splendid new shoes, out of the tree. They said goodbye to him politely, and they went home with their stepmother, arriving just before their father did, so he was none the wiser.

And from that day, they always had a little time to play – their favourite game was leapfrog, and they always hoped that the leprechaun would come along to play with them, but he never did.

And here's the strangest thing – the leprechaun shoes never wore out, and they never became too small for the children's growing feet. They were the most comfortable shoes they had ever worn and they had them for the rest of their lives.

The Magic Bottle

Liam had a little rented house and a small bit of land just outside Cork, where he kept a good milk cow, a pig and some chickens. He and his wife Maeve and their four children were able to live quite well. Then, one spring, the pig died and the chickens got sick and stopped laying eggs. Soon Liam and Maeve were behind with the rent.

After a lot of discussion and sleepless nights, they decided that there was nothing for it but to sell the cow.

'What will we do when she's gone?' wondered Liam.

'I don't know,' said Maeve, sadly, 'but if we don't sell her, we'll be thrown out of our little house. Be sure, though, to get as much money as you can for her, because we'll need every penny.'

So the following Monday, which was fair day, Liam was up early and on the road with the cow, because it was quite a long walk to the fair.

It was a lovely sunny day, and Liam would have enjoyed the walk if his heart hadn't been so heavy at the thought of selling the family's cow. He had just reached the top of a steep hill when he was overtaken by a little man dressed in a very old-fashioned green jacket and breeches, with silver-buckled boots on his feet. He had a wrinkled face, a big thatch of white hair and a pair of twinkling blue eyes dancing above his sharp little nose.

'Good morning,' he said in a cracked voice.

'Good morning to you, sir,' said Liam, thinking that his companion was a bit strange looking.

He drove his cow a little faster along the road,

thinking to get ahead of the little man, but the stranger managed to keep up with him, even though he didn't seem to be making much effort about it. In fact, when Liam looked at him out of the corner of his eye, he seemed to be gliding along the road, although the surface was rough and full of pot-holes.

'Where are you off to with that fine cow?' asked the little man suddenly.

'I'm off to the fair,' replied Liam.

'Are you going to sell her there?'

'Well, now, why else would I be going to the fair with her but to sell her?'

'Would you sell her to me?'

Liam was astonished. The little man was so strange he was afraid to have anything to do with him, but he was also afraid to say no to him. He had to think about what to do.

'What will you pay me for her?' he asked, at last.

'I could give you this bottle,' said the little man, pulling an empty bottle from under his coat.

Liam started laughing, and he laughed so long and so hard that tears were running down his face and he had to hold his sides to stop them splitting.

'A bottle?' he said. 'An empty bottle? Now I know you must be joking. Give you my good cow for a bottle, and an empty bottle at that? Stop holding me back now and I'll be off to the fair to get a good price for my cow.'

'Laugh all you like,' said his companion, who was not a bit put out. 'I can tell you that this bottle is better than any money you might get for your cow at the fair, ten thousand times better.'

'You think I'm going to believe that tall tale?' said Liam. 'Anyway, if I gave you the cow, what would I tell Maeve? And how would we pay the rent?'

'I'm telling you,' said the little man, 'This bottle is better than any money you would get for her. This is your last chance. Take the bottle and give me the cow, Liam O'Connor.'

'How on earth does he know my name?' wondered Liam, while the little man looked at him intently.

'I know you, Liam O'Connor, and I know all about you. How do you know your cow won't die before you get her to the fair? How do you know there'll be a good crowd at the fair and that you'll get a good price for her? Look on this as a final warning. Take it or leave it, but why would you throw your luck away when it's being offered to you on a plate?'

'Oh, no! I would not throw away my luck, sir,' said Liam. 'And if I was sure the bottle was as good as you say, empty or not, I'd give you the cow, and gladly.'

'Just give me the cow, said the little man, impatiently. 'I would not tell you a lie. Just take the bottle, and when you go home, do exactly as I tell you.'

'I don't know …' said Liam, thinking of what Maeve would say if he came home empty-handed except for a bottle with nothing in it.

'Well then, goodbye. I can't wait around for you to make up your mind. Take the bottle and be rich; refuse it and see your children go without and your wife dying in poverty. That will happen to you, Liam O'Connor!' said the little man with a nasty grin.

Liam found it hard not to believe the man, and he reached out for the bottle.

'Take the cow,' he said. 'If you are lying, I curse you.'

'I don't care about your curses, Liam O'Connor, but just do what I tell you and all will be well.'

'And what's that?' asked Liam.

'When you go home, don't mind if your wife is angry with you, but make her sweep the room clean and set the table with a clean cloth over it, then put the bottle on the ground and say these words: "Bottle, do your duty."'

'And is that all?' asked Liam, puzzled.

'That's all there is to it,' said the little man. 'Goodbye, Liam O'Connor – you're a rich man now.'

Liam turned in the road and set off for home. After a few paces, he couldn't help turning back to look after the cow and her purchaser, but they had vanished.

Liam arrived home to a fine welcome from his wife, who was sitting by the fire.

'Oh! Liam, are you back already? What happened to you? Where is the cow? Did you sell her? How much money did you get for her? What news do you have? And what is that bottle under your waistcoat?'

'Well,' said Liam, putting the bottle on the table and feeling a bit foolish. 'This is what I got for the cow.'

His poor wife was thunderstruck. 'And what good is that? I never thought you were such a fool! What on earth will we do for the rent?'

Liam told her his story and Maeve, who had faith in the little people, could not help believing him. She got up, and began to sweep the floor; then she tidied up and spread a clean cloth on the table. Liam put the bottle on the table and said, 'Bottle, do your duty!'

At once, two tiny little fellows rose like light from the bottle, and in an instant they had covered the table with gold and silver dishes, full of the finest food ever seen, then they jumped back into the bottle again.

Liam and Maeve had never seen the like, but when they'd got over the shock, they sat down with the children and ate their fill.

'You'll be a rich man yet, Liam O'Connor,' said Maeve as they made their way to bed.

The next day, Liam went to Cork and sold the beautiful dishes and bought a horse and cart and any number of other things that they needed. The family did all they could to keep the bottle a secret, but even so, the landlord found out about it. He offered Liam a lot of money for it, but Liam refused to give it up, until the man offered to give him the farm in exchange for it. Liam had grown very rich and thought he'd never need any more money, so he gave his landlord the bottle in return for the farm. However, by now he'd got used to being able to buy whatever he wanted, so he went on spending money as if it would never run out.

Of course, soon the family were as poor as they had been before and had nothing left but one cow; and Liam once again drove his cow before him to sell her at the fair, hoping to meet the old man and get another bottle. It was hardly daybreak when he left home, and he walked on at a good pace until he reached the big hill.

Just as soon as he got to the top of the hill, he heard a familiar voice.

'Well, Liam O'Connor, I told you, didn't I, that you would be a rich man.'

'Indeed I was, but I'm not so rich now. I don't suppose you'd have another bottle, for I need it now as much as I did long ago; so if you have it, sir, you can have the cow.'

'And here is the bottle,' said the little man, smiling. 'You know what to do with it. Well, goodbye for ever, Liam O'Connor – you won't be seeing me again. As I told you before, you'll be a rich man, a very rich man, and you'll never have to worry about money again.'

Liam ran home as fast as he could, calling out to Maeve as he went through the door: 'I have another bottle! Get the table ready, quick!'

'You're a lucky man, Liam O'Connor,' said Maeve, bustling around sweeping the floor and laying the cloth on the table.

Liam put the bottle on the table and called out, 'Bottle, do your duty!' Two huge men with cudgels jumped out of the bottle, beat poor Liam and Maeve and the children, then back into the bottle with them.

Once Liam had got over the shock, he thought and thought for a long time and then he swept up the bottle and went to his landlord.

'Well, what do you want now, O'Connor?' he asked crossly. 'You're interrupting a grand feast.'

'Nothing, sir, but I have another bottle.'

'Have you, now? And is it as good as the first?'

'Yes, sir, and better; if you like, I will show you.'

Liam was brought into the great hall, where he saw his old bottle standing high up on a shelf.

Liam set the new bottle on the floor and said the words. In an instant the two huge men were out of the bottle and laying in to everyone in the hall. Glasses and dishes were flying in every direction, and the landlord called on Liam to stop the men and put them back in the bottle.

'I won't make them stop until I get my old bottle back,' said Liam.

'Take it, then, quick, before we're all killed!' shouted the landlord.

Liam's wife took the old bottle down from the shelf and put it under her apron. The two huge men jumped into the new bottle, and husband and wife carried both bottles home. Liam sealed the second bottle and

only ever called the men out of the first bottle. He grew richer than ever and he and Maeve lived a long and happy life together. They both died on the same day.

After their funeral some of the servants got drunk at the wake and broke both bottles. And that was the end of the magic bottles and their luck!

The Three Wishes

It's a well-known fact that all leprechauns have a pot of gold, hidden far, far away from anyone who might want to get their hands on it. However, what isn't so well known (because the leprechauns like to keep their secrets) is that if you can catch a leprechaun and keep eye contact with him, he'll have to grant you three wishes. A few people have managed this, but you have to be very careful not to make a fourth wish on the day that the leprechaun grants your wishes – otherwise you might as well not have met him at all because your three wishes will be cancelled.

Ciarán was walking home one wet evening, wishing that he would meet a leprechaun. His wife was always cross with him because they never had enough money. She had had great notions of grandeur when they got

married. Nothing was good enough for her and nothing he could do was enough for her, even though he worked from sunrise to sunset. She started complaining as soon as he got home in the evenings, and didn't stop until he left the following morning – for all he knew, she complained all day, even when he wasn't there. Ciarán knew exactly what he would wish for if he found a leprechaun, and he knew that he wouldn't be stupid enough to make an extra wish on the same day – when he had his wishes granted, he wouldn't need anything else!

So there he was, striding home along the muddy road, the hedges and trees dripping all around him, when he thought he saw something glowing behind a hedge. He crept through the hedge and there, sitting cross-legged on a stool beside a lantern, was a little man in breeches and a red jacket, stitching away at a tiny pair of red

shoes no bigger than your little fingernail. The little
fellow was concentrating so hard on what he was doing
that he didn't even notice Ciarán until Ciarán had put
out his hand and grabbed him firmly by the collar.

'Put me down! Put me down at once!' shrieked the
little man angrily.

'I will when you've given me three wishes,' said Ciarán, 'for I know you have it in your power to do so.'

'Now, where did you hear that?' asked the little man. 'Sure I'm only a poor cobbler, working for my living, same as anyone else.'

'No human person could fit into those shoes you're stitching,' retorted Ciarán, 'so I know you're one of the little people. Now, give me my three wishes, then I'll let you go and be on my way.'

'Oh, all right, so,' said the little man sulkily. 'Get on with it, then. What is your dearest wish?'

'I'd like a big house, as big as a castle, with bedrooms for all my children, fine furniture and clothes to please my wife and lots of servants.'

'Is that so?' said the leprechaun, for that is what he was. 'That sounds like four wishes to me.'

'No,' said Ciarán, 'it isn't, because I didn't take a breath while I was asking. I know a thing or two about this wishing lark.'

'I suppose you're right,' grumbled the leprechaun. 'What else do you want?'

'I'd like a thousand acres of land around the house, very rich farmland with lots of head of prime cattle grazing on it.'

'Right so,' said the leprechaun. 'I can hear the cattle lowing already. You'll need to get them in for the m...'

'And for my third wish,' interrupted Ciarán, 'I want a pot of gold that never empties.'

'Always the pot of gold,' said the leprechaun crossly. 'Is that all you humans ever think about? Well, it's yours. Now let go of me and leave me in peace.'

Ciarán let go of the leprechaun and the little man disappeared. He rubbed his eyes, wondering if he'd daydreamed everything, and then he saw a tiny red shoe on the ground beside him.

He raced home as fast as he good, bursting with the news of his good fortune. When he got to his cottage there was a fine carriage standing outside the front door, with four beautiful horses champing at the bit in the traces.

'Bríd, Bríd!' he shouted, bursting through the front door. 'You won't believe what just happened!'

'I would so,' said Bríd, appearing from the kitchen with the children in tow. 'We're all getting ready to set out for the new house.'

So they all climbed into the carriage, settled back on the soft cushions and Ciarán tapped the roof so the coachman would know to set off. And off they went, flying through the countryside until they reached a huge house at the end of a long drive lined with grazing cattle. In they went and the servants took their coats and led them into a big dining room, the table groaning under the weight of all the food.

'I want to see what this house has to offer before we settle down to a meal,' said Bríd, and off with her up the stairs. 'Let's see if the leprechaun was as good as his word.'

Ciarán followed her slowly, looking into all the rooms and finally finding what he was looking for. There, in the middle of an empty room, was a big cauldron filled to overflowing with shining gold coins. He had just plunged his hands into the cauldron, hardly able to believe his good fortune, when Bríd bustled in, bursting with indignation.

'Well,' she said 'it's all very well filling my wardrobe with fine clothes, but there isn't a stitch for the children. How can they look as fine as they should with no new clothes?'

'Hush, woman,' said Ciarán. 'Can't you see that we have a big pot of gold here, one that will never run out? We can buy whatever we like with it.'

'I don't see why we should have to spend any of that on what's rightfully ours – you should have made better arrangements with that leprechaun,' complained Bríd. 'You never think things through!'

'Oh, for goodness' sake!' shouted Ciarán, losing his patience. 'Just for once, I wish you could be happy with what you've got!'

Suddenly, everything went dark, and Ciarán felt himself whirling round and round until he landed with a bump on the ground. Bríd and the children were scattered all around him in the middle of an empty field and there was no sign of a house, or a carriage, or any cattle – just the long road home winding its way over the hill.

As they picked themselves up and went sadly on their way back to their cottage, Ciarán was sure he could hear someone laughing in the distance.

The Wedding

Conor McCarthy was struggling through the wind and rain one evening, battling his way up the hill that led to his home.

'A nice hot drink would be just the thing,' he thought. 'I wish I had a nice hot toddy in my hands right now.'

'Never wish it twice,' said a voice. Conor looked up, and there in front of him was a little man, wearing an old-fashioned green coat and breeches, a hat set at a jaunty angle and boots with shiny gold buckles. He was holding a steaming mug of hot toddy, which he gave to Conor, who took it and drained it without taking a breath, warming his hands on the outside of the mug all the while.

'Thank you,' said Conor. 'That was just what I needed on a raw night like tonight.'

'You're welcome,' said the little man, 'but you must get out your purse now and pay me.'

'Pay you, is it?' shouted Conor. 'Why should I pay you? I could just as easily put you in my pocket and take you home with me.'

'You don't know who you're dealing with, Conor McCarthy,' said the stranger angrily. 'You will pay me by being my servant for the next seven years.'

At once, Conor was sorry that he had crossed the little man, but when the stranger turned and walked up the hill, he felt that he had to follow him. They spent the night travelling up hill and down dale, through hedges and ditches and over bogs and meadows.

At daybreak, the little man turned to Conor and said, 'You can go home now, but be sure to meet me on the road tonight. If you're a good servant, I'll be a good master, of that you can be sure.'

Conor went home, but he didn't get a wink of sleep, wondering what tasks the strange little man would have for him. When evening fell, he made his way to the road again and met his new master.

'We are going on a journey tonight,' said he, 'so you'll need to saddle up two horses, one for me and one for yourself.'

'But where is your stable?' asked Conor, looking around him. He could see nothing but the road and the fields and a river running along the bottom of them.

'Ask no questions,' said the little man. 'Go and pluck two rushes from the river bank, and bring them to me.'

Puzzled, Conor did as he'd been told and came back with two fine rushes.

The little man straddled one of them. 'Hup! Hup! Conor, get up on your horse!' he ordered.

'What horse?' asked Conor, wondering what was going on – it was the strangest night he'd ever spent, and it was about to get stranger still.

'It's the best horse you'll ever have ridden,' said the little man, holding out the second rush.

'You must be mad,' muttered Conor, but he straddled the rush, just as he had been ordered.

'Borram! Borram! Borram!' shouted the little man and, suddenly, both servant and master were sitting astride fine horses. Conor had been a bit careless about where he had placed himself, and he was facing the horse's tail when it galloped off. As a result, he spent the whole journey holding on to the animal's tail for dear life.

They rode for a long time, and when they finally stopped, it was outside a large, well-lit public house.

'In we go,' said the little man, 'but seeing as you can't tell the head of a horse from its tail, say nothing when you've had a few drinks.'

Conor went in and they both sat beside the fire and drank their fill, and then they set off back the way they'd come. Conor went home, having promised the little man to meet him the following night.

The next night, the same thing happened, but on the third night, when Conor met the little man, he told him to bring three rushes from the river bank, as they'd have need of a third horse that night to bring someone back with them.

Off they rode, leading the third horse behind them, and finally stopped outside a cosy farmhouse.

'I'm a thousand years old today,' said the little man, 'and I'm minded to take a wife. There's a fine young girl in this house who's about to get married and I'll take her for myself if she sneezes three times before the night is over.'

'Will you now?' thought Conor, thinking what a miserable thing it would be for a fine young girl to marry a wizened old leprechaun. 'Not if I can help it.'

Into the farmhouse they went and the wedding party was feasting and merry-making – the wedding itself would take place later that night when the priest had eaten and drunk his fill. The bride was indeed a fine young woman, with clear creamy skin and long black hair like a raven's wing.

The leprechaun disappeared into the roof and found himself a comfortable place to sit on a beam. Conor mingled and had a good feed and a few drinks.

During the feast, some pepper got up the bride's nose and she sneezed – everyone had a mouth filled with food, so no one blessed her to jinx the sneeze.

'One,' Conor heard the little man saying from his beam high up in the roof.

Soon afterwards, a latecomer came through the door and a gust of wind raised some dust from the hearth. The bride sneezed again – and again nobody blessed her to jinx the sneeze.

'Two,' Conor heard from the roof.

About half an hour later, Conor saw a little white cat jump under the table and walk through all the legs until she came to the bride's chair, then she sat down underneath it. The poor girl must have been allergic to cats, for didn't she give a huge sneeze?

'Thr...'

'Bless you!' shouted Conor, finally jinxing the sneeze. The little man jumped down from the beam, his face dark with fury, and gave Conor a kick that sent him sprawling across the table.

'Take that as my reward for your service,' he shouted, and disappeared in a puff of smoke.

By then, the priest had feasted to his satisfaction and was now ready to marry the happy couple, which he did with no further delay.

Conor walked home in the early hours when the wedding celebrations had finally come to an end. His head was full of the night's events, and cold though the night was, he never once wished for a hot toddy.

The Magic Thread

Tadhg was driving his cattle home for milking one fine evening, when he heard a gentle tapping sound coming from the thick hedgerow along the side of the road.

'That's odd,' he said to himself. 'I don't think I've ever heard an animal making that sort of noise.'

Leaving the cattle to make their own way home, he crept up to the hedgerow and parted the bushes – lo and behold, what did he see only a tiny little man dressed in green, tapping away at the sole of a shoe with the smallest hammer imaginable.

'Well, hello,' he said, startling the little man, who almost fell off the old tin can he was sitting on. 'And who might you be?'

'None of your business,' retorted the little man. 'Now, why don't you go away and leave me to mine?'

But Tadhg's mind was working overtime, remembering all the tales his granny had told him about the little people, particularly the leprechauns and their crocks of gold. Wouldn't a crock of gold coins be a big help to him?

'I don't think I'll do that,' he replied, and his hand reached out to grab the little man firmly by the wrist. 'I know what you are, and now you're going to take me to your gold.'

'What gold?' said the little man. 'I don't know what you think I am, but you're very much mistaken if it's anything other than a hardworking cobbler.'

'You don't fool me,' said Tadhg. 'I know you're a leprechaun, and I'm going to have your gold.'

By this time, Tadhg's cattle were almost home, and he knew he needed to catch up with them. But what could he do with the leprechaun? He didn't think he could milk the cattle and keep an eye on him, and everyone knew that if you took your eyes off a leprechaun, he'd be off in a flash.

He looked around the field, and then he had a brainwave. He had heard that one of the only things a leprechaun couldn't escape from was a plough chain, and there, in the farthest corner of the field, was an ancient rusty plough, rattling in the breeze, with nettles growing through it. Keeping his eyes and a good grip on the leprechaun, he ran over to the plough and there, sure enough, was the chain, rusty but strong. Tadhg wrapped it twice around the little man's waist and hooked it up to the plough.

'Now,' he said, 'you wait here. I have to go and

milk my cows, but I'll be back soon and then you can take me to your gold.'

The leprechaun was shaking with rage, but he knew he'd met his match, so he settled down to wait for his captor to return from the milking.

By the time Tadhg had finished the milking, it was dark. He'd been thinking about the leprechaun and was wondering how he could detach the chain from the plough so that he could be sure that his prisoner wouldn't escape while they went in search of the crock of gold. He thought and thought, and then he had another brainwave! Wasn't his wife always at the knitting – jumpers, cardigans, hats, scarves – balls and balls of wool she had, mostly red, all around the house? And the only other thing that a leprechaun couldn't escape from was a woollen thread.

Tadhg ran into the house, calling out to his wife.

'Aoife! Aoife! Where are you?'

'I'm in the attic,' came the muffled reply. 'What is it? Your dinner won't be ready for half an hour.'

'Forget dinner,' shouted Tadhg, running up the

stairs. 'What I need from you now is a ball of wool – where do you keep them?'

'A ball of wool? What on earth do you need a ball of wool for …? Oh, look it, just get one out of the chest of drawers in the hall and let me get on with my sorting out up here.'

Tadhg raced down the stairs again and opened the top drawer in the hall chest. Sure enough, there was a huge selection of balls of red wool, neatly arranged in order of size.

'Well,' thought Tadhg, 'I just need a small amount of wool to attach to the leprechaun's wrist and mine. It doesn't have to be very thick – the magic will work anyway.'

And he picked up a small ball of fine wool, still in its wrapper.

Picking up a shovel, and a lamp, because it was now getting dark, Tadhg left the house and hurried down the road to the field where he had left the leprechaun. He wasn't sure if the magic of the chain was just another story or if it actually worked, so he was half expecting the leprechaun to have vanished. But no, there he was, sitting on the ground, legs crossed, grumbling.

'I thought you'd never get back,' he whined to Tadhg. 'I suppose you stopped to have your dinner, and not a thought for me.'

'Not at all – I'm as hungry as you are,' retorted Tadhg. 'So let's get on with this, and then we can both have something to eat.'

He tied the end of the ball of wool around the leprechaun's wrist, putting the ball back in his pocket,

and then he released the little man from the chain. Off they went, across the fields, the lamp lighting their way in the darkness.

'It's just as well I have the wool,' thought Tadhg. 'I wouldn't be able to keep my eye on the leprechaun on this moonless night.'

Dawn was breaking by the time the leprechaun stopped. They were at the edge of a large field, bordered by hawthorn trees.

'Is this where your crock of gold is, then?' asked Tadhg.

'It is,' said the leprechaun, 'under that hawthorn tree.' He waved vaguely in the direction of the corner of the field. 'And if you knew how hard I'd worked to gather it, you wouldn't be thinking of stealing it.'

'Stop your moaning,' said Tadhg, putting his lamp

on the ground. The ground was uneven and the lamp fell over, so he turned around to set it right. He felt a tug on the ball of wool in his pocket, and when he looked up the leprechaun had disappeared, leaving a trail of red wool behind him. As he heard a faint cackling coming from the distance he reached into his pocket – all that was left of the ball of wool was the wrapper. He turned it over and read the description on the back – 100% cotton.

Tadhg dug deep under every hawthorn tree in that field, but, as you might expect, he found nothing. He trudged home, bitterly disappointed to have lost his one chance of getting rich.

Oisín and the Magic Ball

One hot summer's day, Oisín was sitting on the swing in his back garden, bored because his friends had all gone on holiday.

As he looked around the garden, something caught his eye at the edge of one of the flowerbeds. He jumped off the swing and ran towards the object, which turned out to be a small ball, covered with red and green stripes that looked as if they would glow in the dark. Oisín bent down to pick it up and it rolled further into the undergrowth. He followed it, scratching his arms and legs on his father's prize roses. When it got to the garden wall, the ball hopped over it, and Oisín decided to follow it.

The ball raced off up the field behind Oisín's house, with Oisín running behind it.

'Catch me if you can, catch me if you can …'

Was he dreaming, or was the ball talking to him? Oisín looked all around, but he couldn't see anyone else. He began to run after the ball again, but whenever he got close enough to pick it up, it began to speed up, bouncing along the grass.

At the edge of the meadow there was a stile, and the ball stopped underneath it.

'At last!' breathed Oisín. 'Perhaps it can't bounce high enough to get over the stile, so I'll be able to get it.'

He ran up to the stile, but, just as he got there, the ball bounced up and over it, leaving Oisín struggling to get over the stile. When he landed on the other side, the ball was disappearing into the distance. He thought he could hear someone chanting:

'Catch me if you can, catch me if you can …'

But when he looked around, he could see no one, and thought that perhaps the ball was calling to him as it raced away from him. He ran and ran, but the ball managed to keep well ahead of him.

'Oh, I'll never catch it,' said Oisín. 'Perhaps I should just give up and go home.'

And then he saw that the ball had stopped again, at the top of the hill.

'I think it's playing a game with me,' said Oisín to himself. 'I've nothing better to do, so I might as well go along with it.'

So he ran after ball again, but as soon as he got close to it, it started moving again, bouncing in and out of the long grass, always managing to keep just out of Oisín's reach.

As he got closer to the river, Oisín thought the ball might bounce into the water and he wondered if he should follow it. But he didn't know how to swim and his mother was always warning him about the river. As if it had read his mind, the ball bounced along the bank until it reached a bridge, and then it bounced along the bridge, with Oisín in hot pursuit. The ball stopped dead when it got to the other side.

'It's as if it's waiting for me,' said Oisín to himself. He was beginning to feel quite tired, so he walked towards the ball. As soon as he came within reach of it, it took off again, bouncing along the path through the field. It suddenly veered off, bouncing towards a stand of tall poppies, just like the ones Oisín's mother grew in her garden, but much, much bigger. Oisín stopped to pick some, thinking that his mother would be pleased, and then he realised that the ball was on

the move again, this time heading towards some trees. Picking up the poppies he'd gathered, he followed the ball once again. This time, when the ball stopped, it didn't move again, and Oisín was finally able to get close enough to pick it up.

The ball was warm in his hand, and it felt almost as if it was alive. 'That's odd,' thought Oisín, 'it doesn't feel like any ball I've ever held before.'

He bounced it gently off the ground – there was a loud pop and the ball disappeared.

'I must have burst it,' thought Oisín, 'but I didn't bounce it all that hard.'

Sadly, he decided to set off home again. When he turned, standing in front of him was the smallest man he'd ever seen, all dressed in green, wearing a tall hat adorned with a black band that matched his belt.

'Who are you?' whispered Oisín, although the little man looked just like the leprechauns in his storybooks. But this little man was smiling, and Oisín knew from the stories that leprechauns didn't like humans and would sometimes go out of their way to make trouble for them.

'Are you a leprechaun?' he asked.

'I am,' said the little man. 'My name is Róló,' he

continued, climbing onto a toadstool. 'You've just followed me here from your garden.'

'But I followed a ball,' said Oisín, puzzled.

The little man made himself comfortable on his toadstool, crossing his legs and taking out a pipe and lighting it before he spoke again.

'Well, then,' he said 'it seems that I have you to thank for breaking the spell.'

'What spell?' asked Oisín, pinching himself on the arm, because nothing that was happening seemed very real to him.

'I was put under a spell by a wicked witch and the spell could only be broken if someone bounced me inside a fairy ring. As soon as you did that, the spell was broken.'

Oisín looked down and saw that he was standing just outside a ring of toadstools, although he hadn't noticed them before.

'Was that why you made me follow you?' he asked.

'Well, I hoped you would,' said Róló. 'I've been trying to get out of that ball for three years.'

'Three years!' said Oisín. 'That's a very long time to be stuck inside a ball. How did you get in there?'

'I'll tell you what happened, if you like, and then I'll grant you one wish as a reward for freeing me. But you'll have to step inside the fairy ring, otherwise the magic won't work properly and I won't be able to grant you a wish.'

So Oisín stepped inside the fairy ring and waited for Róló to tell him his story.

'There was an old witch hereabouts,' began Róló. 'She was so nasty that nobody liked her. One day, she was riding along on her broomstick when, suddenly, it snapped, and she fell off and landed on top of that hill over there. I was sitting at the bottom of the hill, mending shoes. She rolled down the hill until she was at my feet. Her hair had bits of grass sticking out of it, and she'd lost a shoe and squashed her pointy hat on the way down. It was so funny that I started to laugh.

'"What are you laughing at?" she shouted.

'"Well," I said, "you just looked so funny rolling down the hill …"

'"Funny, is it?" she snapped. "How would you like to spend the rest of your life rolling around?"

'"Not much," I said, because it really didn't sound like a lot of fun.

'"What's your name?" asked the witch.

'"Róló," I answered, and the witch began to shriek with laughter.

'"Hah! Róló – that's a good name for a rolling ball," she cackled. "So I'm going to turn you into a ball, and you'll only get out again if someone bounces you inside a fairy ring."

'And I was suddenly inside the ball that you followed here. I tried so many times to make someone follow me to the fairy ring, but you're the first person who didn't give up, and for that I thank you.'

'Well, I'm glad I could help,' said Oisín. 'But I've been away from home for a long time and I'd better get back. Everyone will be worried.' And then it occurred to him that he was completely lost. Once he'd crossed over the river, he was in unknown territory.

'I wish I knew how to get home,' he said, forgetting that Róló had offered to grant him a wish.

And the next thing he knew, he was sitting on the swing in his back garden, a bunch of wilted poppies in his hand.

And some people might think that that was a waste of a perfectly good wish, but Oisín didn't, because he had had such an amazing adventure, and he was glad that he had been able to help the leprechaun, who was much nicer than the ones in the stories.

Under the Hawthorn Tree

Clodagh and Cian were mischievous twins, always getting themselves into scrapes, never listening to their parents – in other words, they were Trouble, with a capital T.

One night, when they should have been asleep, they were sitting at the top of the stairs listening to the adults chatting and gossiping and telling stories. They always loved their grandad's stories, so they listened very quietly whenever they heard his voice.

'Of course the little people exist,' they heard him say in his deep, booming voice. He paused to light his pipe – always a lengthy process.

'Why do you think we're so careful not to cut down or damage the hawthorn trees?' he went on. 'It's not as if they all grow in convenient corners of fields. I have three in my top meadow, and it takes ages to work my way around them when I'm ploughing and planting.'

'Aye, I suppose so,' said one of the neighbours, another farmer. 'I'm always careful not to damage them, too.'

'It's that big one in the top meadow that has all the magic,' said Grandad. 'I wouldn't be surprised if there was a big crock of gold under it.'

'Wouldn't it be nice to get your hands on that?' chortled the twins' Uncle Domhnall. 'I'd say they'd have it protected with any number of spells and charms and what have you.'

At the mention of gold, the twins' eyes widened until they were as round as saucers. They were often able to read each other's minds, and an interesting plan was taking shape …

Off they went to bed again, full of excitement about what the next day would bring.

The following morning, the twins were so excited they could hardly eat their breakfast – they couldn't wait to go outside and put their plan into action.

'What's up with you two this morning?' asked Grandad. 'I hope you're not planning any of your usual mischief today.'

'Oh, no, Grandad,' they replied together. 'We just want to play outside. We've thought of a new game and we're going to try it out.'

Grandad was a bit suspicious, but he had other concerns that day, and he soon forgot about his grandchildren's plans.

After breakfast, the twins went outside and headed up to Grandad's top meadow, Clodagh leading the way, as she often did. They had a steep climb to the top of the meadow, where they settled down behind a bush to watch and wait. Several hours later, nothing had happened, and they were beginning to feel hungry, so they ran down the hill for some lunch. After lunch, they went back to the meadow again, and took up their lookout position again. Nothing happened all afternoon, and they went home, a bit disappointed, but not discouraged.

For almost a week, the twins went out to the meadow every day. Nobody paid much attention to them, glad that for once they weren't causing trouble, as they usually did in the long summer holidays.

Then, one afternoon, just as they were about to call it a day, their patience was finally rewarded. Walking up the meadow towards the big hawthorn tree, what did they see, only a leprechaun! He had his cobbling tools in a little sack that he was carrying over his shoulder, and he was whistling a jolly little tune.

With Clodagh in the lead again, the twins ran up behind him, as quietly as they could, and they were

certain he hadn't seen them. When he slipped under the tree, they were right behind him, and they followed him down the twisted route that he had taken. Down, down they went, eventually landing with a bump on the ground underneath the tree.

They were dusting themselves down when they saw that the leprechaun was behind them, covering up the entrance to the underground chamber.

'So,' he said. 'You've found us out, finally. Aren't you the clever pair? Well, now you're here, you'd better have a look around the place. Although …' he added threateningly, 'perhaps you'll find yourselves wishing you hadn't been so curious.'

Clodagh and Cian gulped, feeling a bit worried. Had they gone too far this time?

'Now,' said the leprechaun briskly, 'is there anything

in particular you'd like to see while you're here?'

'Well,' said Cian. 'We've heard that you might have a big crock of gold down here. We'd love to see that!'

'Would you, indeed?' smiled the leprechaun. 'Well, why don't you have something to eat first, and then we'll see about this crock of gold?'

He led them into the next chamber, which was furnished with a great big dining table and lots of chairs. There was a leprechaun in every seat, and they were all tucking in to the huge number of different dishes on the table. Sparkling chandeliers above the table lit the scene.

The leprechauns may have been surprised to see Clodagh and Cian, but they remembered their manners and pulled up two more chairs to the table. The twins were invited to sit down and all manner of delicious things were served up to them.

'What brings you to our magic tree?' asked one of the leprechauns.

'Well,' answered Clodagh, 'people are always talking about the little people and all the gold they have, and we wanted to see it for ourselves.'

'Is that so?' laughed the leprechaun. 'I'm sure your family would be delighted if you went back to them with a crock of gold.'

'They certainly would!' said Cian. 'We're always in trouble, but this would make everyone very pleased with us.'

The food kept coming and the leprechauns kept eating, long after the twins had had enough. Then the table was cleared and pushed back against the wall and the leprechauns started dancing to lovely music that seemed to be coming from behind the walls. This went on for hours and hours, and the children began to wonder what would happen next. They remembered what the first leprechaun had said and they were beginning to feel a bit afraid. They decided to go looking for him in the crowd of merrymaking leprechauns. Finally, they spotted him in the throng.

'We'd quite like to go home now,' they said politely.

'It's a bit late in the day for that,' he said. 'Don't you want to see the gold?' he asked.

'Well, yes, we do ...' said Clodagh, 'but perhaps we could do it another time? We really have to be getting back. Everyone will be getting worried about us.'

'All right, so,' said the leprechaun. 'I'll show you the way out, but only if you promise never to tell anyone what you've seen here.'

'We promise, we promise!' chorused the twins, who wanted nothing more than to get back to their nice ordinary lives.

'And you'll both mend your ways and stop worrying everyone,' added the leprechaun, for good measure.

'We will, we will!' they cried.

The little people crowded around, saying goodbye to the twins, shaking their hands and wishing them well, then the leprechaun led them back to the chamber under the roots of the tree and showed them how to climb out into the world again.

They climbed up, up, up, and they suddenly found themselves in the top meadow again. But it had just been ploughed, and the grass hadn't even been cut when they had followed the leprechaun under the tree. There was a fresh breeze blowing, although it had been hot and hazy earlier that day. All the way home, the landscape had changed – there was blossom on all the trees, even though it was late summer. What on earth was going on?

After fifteen minutes, they arrived at the door of their farmhouse. It opened just as they were about to

turn the handle, and there was Grandad, looking at them as if he couldn't believe his eyes.

'Sally! Tim!' he called. 'Come quickly!' The twins' parents were suddenly beside him.

'Where have you been?' they asked. 'We thought you must have drowned in the lake – we've been looking for you everywhere!'

'But we've only been gone a few hours,' said Clodagh, puzzled. 'We've just come back for tea.'

'A few hours!' said her mother. 'You've been gone for months. We thought you were dead. Where on earth have you been?'

But the twins remembered their promise to the leprechaun and they said nothing, although their Grandad was looking at them a bit strangely.

They soon settled back into their lives and went back to school, where they had a lot of catching up to do, and they never, ever, told anyone about their adventure under the hawthorn tree.

Sometimes, when they were out playing in the meadow, they would see the leprechaun making his way home, whistling his little tune, but they would just wave at him and go back to their game.

And people remarked about how the twins' behaviour had changed. They always said where they were going and they were happy to help around the house and farm – and they no longer stuck their noses into everyone else's business.

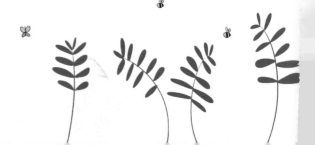

Pronunciation Guide

I rish names and words can look very strange, with lots of silent consonants and accents on vowels. To complicate things, some words are pronounced differently depending on which region of Ireland the speaker comes from. This handy phonetic guide will show you how the names and words you come across in this book are usually pronounced.

Aoife	*Ee-fah*
bothán (a shed)	*buhawn*
Bríd	*Breed*
Caomhín	*Quee-veen*
Cathal	*Ka-hal*
Cian	*Kee-ann*

Ciarán	*Keer-awn*
Clodagh	*Clow-dah*
Cormac	*Kor-mock*
Darach	*Dah-rah*

Deirdre	*Deer-drah*
Diarmuid	*Deer-mwid*
Domhnall	*Doh-nal*
Eithne	*Eth-na*
Eoin	*Owen*
Feargal	*Fur-gal*
feadóg (a tin whistle)	*fah-dogue*
Fiachra	*Fee-ack-ra*
Fionnuala	*Finn-oola*
lios (a fairy fort)	*liss*
Maeve	*Mave*
Lorcan	*Lore-kan*
Mícheál	*Mee-hawl*
Niall	*Nee-ahl*

Pronunciation Guide

Oisín	*Ush-een*
Oonagh	*Oon-ah*
Orla	*Ore-lah*
Pádraig	*Pawd-rick*
Róló	*Roh-low*
Seamas	*Shamus*
Seán	*Shawn*
Sinéad	*Shin-ade*
Tadhg	*Tygue*